# STRANGE HOUSES

# STRANGE HOUSES

# UKETSU

Translated from the Japanese by Jim Rion

HARPERVIA

*An Imprint of* HarperCollins*Publishers*

HENNA IE. Copyright © 2021 by Uketsu. English translation copyright © 2025 by Jim Rion. English translation rights arranged with Futabasha Publishers Ltd. through Japan UNI Agency, Inc., Tokyo, and Pushkin Press Limited. A Note from the Translator © 2025 by Jim Rion. All rights reserved. Printed in the United States of America. No part of this book may be used or reproduced in any manner whatsoever without written permission except in the case of brief quotations embodied in critical articles and reviews. Without limiting the author's and publisher's exclusive rights, any unauthorized use of this publication to train generative artificial intelligence (AI) technologies is expressly prohibited. For information, address HarperCollins Publishers, 195 Broadway, New York, NY 10007.

HarperCollins books may be purchased for educational, business, or sales promotional use. For information, please email the Special Markets Department at SPsales@harpercollins.com.

Originally published as *HENNA IE* in Japan in 2021 by Futabasha Publishers Ltd., Tokyo. All rights reserved.

FIRST HARPERVIA EDITION PUBLISHED IN 2025

*Design adapted from the UK edition designed and typeset by Tetragon, London.*

Library of Congress Cataloging-in-Publication Data has been applied for.

ISBN 978-0-06-343315-1
ISBN 978-0-06-346808-5 (Simultaneous Hardcover Edition)

25 26 27 28 29 LBC 5 4 3 2 1

CV 03.27.2025 1014

# STRANGE HOUSES

Sink

Room

Shower

Toilet

Bed

Stairs

Child's room

Dressing room

Balcony

Shelves

Bath

Bed

Shelves

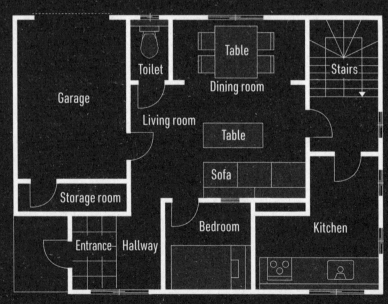

Toilet

Table

Stairs

Dining room

Garage

Living room

Table

Sofa

Storage room

Bedroom

Kitchen

Entrance

Hallway

This is the floor plan of a certain house.

Do you see anything strange about it?

At first glance, it probably looks totally normal, like a house anyone might live in. But if you look very closely, you might notice things here and there that seem somehow . . . off. Those 'off' details pile up and link together to lead to one inescapable truth.

A truth so terrifying, you won't want to believe it.

# CONTENTS

# CHAPTER ONE

# A Strange House

## A MESSAGE FROM A FRIEND

I'm a freelance writer, my specialty being stories of the macabre. Given this line of work, lots of people approach me with their personal experiences of the eerie and unpleasant.

Lots of these have to do with houses.

'I keep hearing footsteps on the second floor, even when no one else is home.'

'I can feel someone watching me when I'm alone.'

'There are voices coming from the wardrobe.'

I can't tell you how many people have told me their scary house stories.

But none of them can compare to the houses in this story. These strange, strange houses.

.    .    .

It all started in September 2019. A friend of mine, Yanaoka, messaged me in need of some advice. Yanaoka's a sales representative with an editing and production company. We've known each other for a few years and get together on occasion for dinner.

He told me that he and his wife were expecting their first child, so they had begun to search for their first house. Finding a good family home is hard work, he said, having spent many a late night scrolling through listings. Then, finally, he came across something that looked ideal.

It was a two-storey house in a quiet residential street, near a station but not far from forested hillsides, and although it was officially preowned, it was still very new. The couple went to see it, and it was so spacious and bright that they both fell in love.

But there was one thing on the floor plan that bothered them.

On the first floor, there was a mysterious dead space between the kitchen and living room.

**FIRST FLOOR**

It had no doors, so it was completely inaccessible. The couple asked the realtors for an explanation, but, clueless, they didn't have one to offer. It was nothing that would affect the couple if they lived there, but something about it felt unsettling, so they decided to hold off pursuing the property for the time being.

Yanaoka said he decided to consult with me since I 'know a lot about weird things'. I admit that I did find myself attracted by the words 'mysterious dead space'. But I don't know the first thing about architecture, and I'm not even sure I know how to properly read a floor plan.

So, I decided to get some help.

## KURIHARA

Among my acquaintances is a man named Kurihara. Not only is he a draughtsman with a prestigious architecture firm, but also a fellow fan of horror and mystery stories, so I thought he might be interested in this.

I emailed him the details and a copy of the floor plan Yanaoka had sent, and we decided to talk things over on the phone.

Here is a transcript of our conversation:

AUTHOR: Good to talk to you again, Kurihara. Thanks for taking the time. I know you're busy.

KURIHARA: Not at all. Now, about that floor plan you sent. . . .

AUTHOR: Right! My friend's wondering about that dead space on the first floor. Do you have any idea what it might be?

KURIHARA: Hmm . . . one thing I can confidently say is, it was put there intentionally.

AUTHOR: You think someone wanted it?

KURIHARA: They must have. If you look closely, you can see that it was created by building two walls that otherwise serve no purpose.

15

Those two walls in the kitchen, do you see? Without those, there's no dead space, and the kitchen would have actually been bigger. They actively built walls that made the kitchen smaller. Clearly, the space must have been put there for a reason.

AUTHOR: I see what you mean. So, what do you think they might have needed it for?

KURIHARA: Maybe they had intended it to be a storage space at first. If they had put doors opening onto the living room, it could have been a cupboard; or a set on the kitchen side could have made a pantry. But then maybe they changed their minds, or ran out of money or something, and gave up on the idea.

AUTHOR: I see. Since they were already in the middle of construction, then, you think they just left it there without altering the plan?

KURIHARA: It seems a natural explanation.

AUTHOR: So, there's nothing ominous or creepy about it at all . . .

KURIHARA: I suppose not. It's just . . .

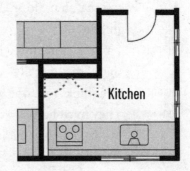

16

Kurihara's tone suddenly turned sombre.

KURIHARA: Do you know who had this house built?

AUTHOR: The previous owners. I heard it was a family of three, a couple with a small child.

KURIHARA: Small . . . how small? Do you know how old the child was?

AUTHOR: I'm afraid I didn't ask. What's that got to do with anything?

KURIHARA: To tell the truth, I thought there was something seriously off about this house the moment I saw the plan.

AUTHOR: You did? What? I didn't notice anything, apart from that dead space.

KURIHARA: The second floor is all wrong. Look at the child's room. Do you notice anything odd about it?

AUTHOR: Well . . . wait, hold on a minute.

## SECOND FLOOR

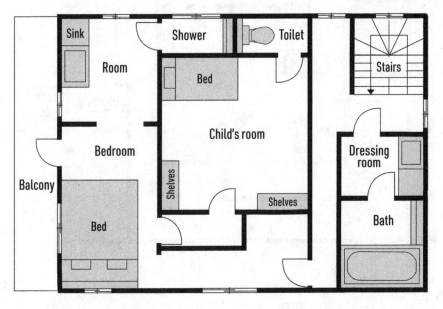

17

I finally understood what he was getting at.

AUTHOR: There are two doors, with a small hallway between!

KURIHARA: Exactly. The child's room has a vestibule outside the door, which is very unusual for a private home.

And the location of the entrance to that child's room is strange, too. If you came up from the first floor, you'd have to walk all the way around to the other side of the house to get to the kid's room. Why make it so much trouble?

AUTHOR: That is odd.

KURIHARA: And the room doesn't have a single window.

 = Door

I immediately saw he was right. There were no windows marked on the floor plan.

KURIHARA: Most parents want their child's room to be as bright and sunny as possible. I don't think I've ever seen a child's room without windows. Not in a single-family home, at least.

AUTHOR: I wonder what the reasoning was. Do you think maybe the child had some kind of skin disease that meant they couldn't be exposed to sunlight, or something like that?

KURIHARA: They could have just put up curtains if that was the case. It's just so odd that they planned a room without a single window at all.

AUTHOR: I agree.

KURIHARA: And there's something else about the room that bothers me. See that toilet? With the door right there, it's only accessible from the child's room.

AUTHOR: You're right. So, it's an en-suite child's room.

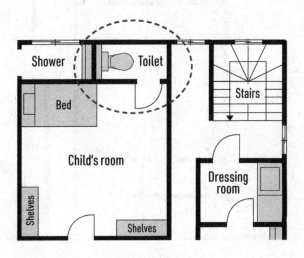

KURIHARA: It is.

AUTHOR: A room with no windows, a double-door vestibule and its own toilet. . . . It's almost like some kind of solitary confinement cell.

KURIHARA: This all goes a bit beyond 'overprotective'. It feels like they were obsessed with keeping the child under complete control. They might have actually locked the kid in there.

AUTHOR: Do you suspect abuse?

KURIHARA: It's possible. If we follow that train of thought, then I might almost say the parents didn't want anyone to know the child was there.

Look at the overall second-floor layout. Doesn't it look like everything else is arranged to hide the

## SECOND FLOOR

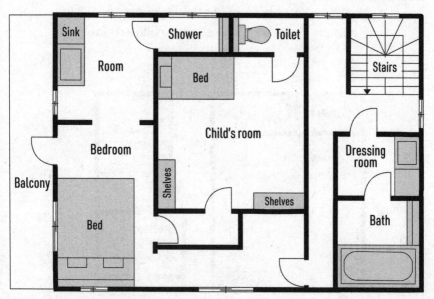

child's room? Of course, without windows, it's not like anyone could see the kid anyway.

The parents kept the child locked in that room and hid their existence completely. That's what I think.

AUTHOR: But why would they do that?

KURIHARA: Who knows? But if I'm reading this floor plan right, there was something very strange going on with that family.


## TWO BATHROOMS

KURIHARA: Also, look at that bedroom next to the child's room.

AUTHOR: There's a double bed in there. Do you think it's the parents' room?

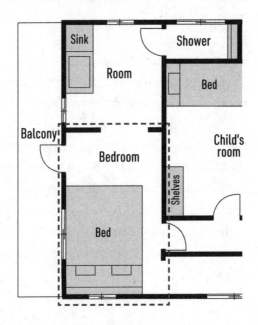

KURIHARA: I'd imagine so. Unlike the child's room, it's really open and airy. It's got lots of windows, see?

I recalled Yanaoka talking about the house being 'spacious and bright'.

KURIHARA: There's something that bothers me about this room, too. There's a shower near the top of the layout. That would mean the neighbouring room doubles as a kind of dressing room. But then, that dressing room would be totally visible from the bedroom.

AUTHOR: You're right, there's no door between them.

KURIHARA: Even married couples want a bit of privacy after a shower. They must have been close. The contrast between being a 'close couple' and having a 'child prisoner' is quite creepy. Of course, I might just be overthinking it.

AUTHOR: Yeah . . . hmm.

KURIHARA: Is something the matter?

AUTHOR: They've got a bathroom and then a separate shower booth in a completely different place on the same floor, too. Isn't that odd?

KURIHARA: It's not unheard of, but also not something you see every day. But . . . this bathroom has no windows, while there's a large one in the shower room.

AUTHOR: You're right. . . .

It's rather an unsettling house in general, isn't it? Well, do you think my friend should hold off from buying it?

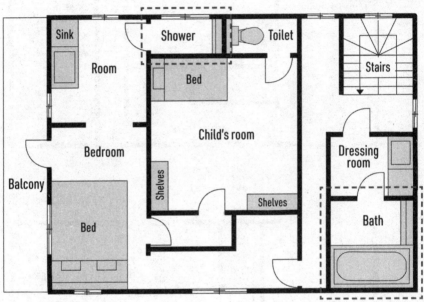

SECOND FLOOR

Sink

Room

Shower

Toilet

Stairs

Bed

Child's room

Bedroom

Dressing room

Shelves

Balcony

Shelves

Bath

Bed

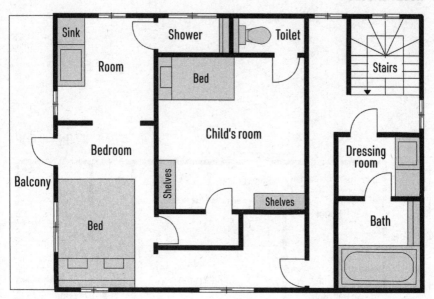

Sink

Room

Shower

Toilet

Bed

Child's room

Bedroom

Balcony

Shelves

Shelves

Stairs

Dressing room

Bath

Bed

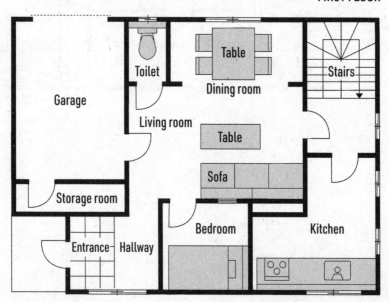

Garage

Toilet

Table

Dining room

Stairs

Living room

Table

Sofa

Storage room

Bedroom

Kitchen

Entrance

Hallway

KURIHARA:  It's hard to say anything for sure just from the layout,
           but if it were me, I wouldn't.

I thanked Kurihara and hung up the phone.

I looked over the floor plan again. My imagination ran wild. A
child trapped in a windowless room. Parents sleeping peacefully
nearby in their big double bed.

I compared the layouts of the two floors. It would be a fairly
normal house if you only looked at the first floor. Apart from
that mysterious dead space, of course. And what about that?
Kurihara called it an unfinished storage space, but was that the
real explanation?

Then, a new idea arose unbidden from the depths of my mind.
A ridiculous one. Even as it occurred to me, I was already telling
myself it was simply too out there. Still . . . I had to make sure. I
laid the two floor plans over each other.

Defying all reason, they supported my new hypothesis
perfectly.

It must be a coincidence, I thought. Or perhaps not . . .

## THE MYSTERIOUS SPACE

I called Kurihara again.

AUTHOR:    I'm sorry to keep bothering you.
KURIHARA:  Not at all. Is there a new development?
AUTHOR:    I just couldn't stop thinking about that dead space. I
           was thinking, what if it had something to do with the
           second-floor layout?

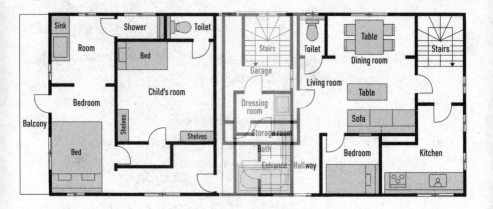

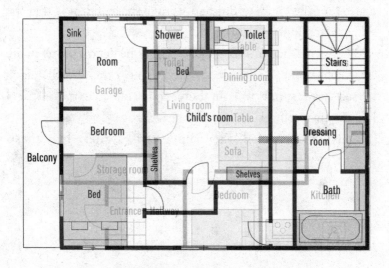

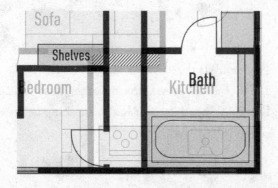

KURIHARA: Really?

AUTHOR: So, I laid the first- and second-floor plans over each other. That dead space aligns perfectly with the corners of the child's room and the bathroom. Like it could be some kind of tunnel between them.

KURIHARA: Ahh . . . I see it now. You're right.

AUTHOR: Could that . . . I mean, I'm no expert at reading floor plans, but could it be that the first-floor space is some kind of passageway?

There could be a hole in the floor of the child's room, and another leading up into the bathroom. This space on the first floor could connect them both. I think, then, the child could pass between the sealed room and the bathroom through the passage. The parents were hiding the existence of their child.

Think about it. Whenever the child went to take a bath, they'd have to pass through a windowed corridor and there would be a risk of them being spotted. So, the parents built a hidden passage connecting the child's room to the bathroom, then the child could take a bath without being seen. And then they put a set of shelves in the child's room over the hole to hide it. Or, at least, that's what I was thinking. What do you say?

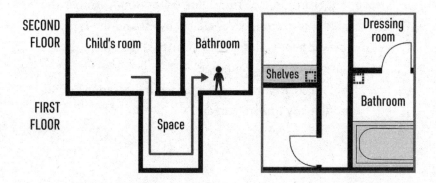

KURIHARA:  Hmm . . . well, it's an interesting idea, I'll give you that.

AUTHOR:  A bit much?

KURIHARA:  I just don't think they'd have to go to such lengths.

AUTHOR:  You're right. Sorry. It just came to me all of a sudden. Forget I said anything.

I was suddenly embarrassed at how sure I'd been. Clearly, my thoughts had strayed too far from reality. Just when I was trying to escape from the conversation, though, I heard Kurihara mumbling to himself.

KURIHARA:  A passage . . . wait, hold on there. If that's the case, then this room . . .

AUTHOR:  What's wrong?

KURIHARA:  I think your theory has some merit, actually. . . . So, you said the previous owners were a family of three, right? Husband, wife and a small child?

AUTHOR:  Yes!

KURIHARA:  Then, there's one bed too many. The couple were sleeping in the bedroom on the second floor. The child sleeps in the child's room. But whose bedroom is this on the first floor?

AUTHOR:  Hmm. Maybe a guest room, for when visitors stay over? Something like that?

KURIHARA:  I suppose that must be it. People must have come to stay, from time to time. But, by putting together the guests, the windowless child's room and the separate shower room, along with your passage idea, I think I start to see a story emerge.

    I mean, it's pretty outlandish, but if you don't mind, indulge my little daydream.

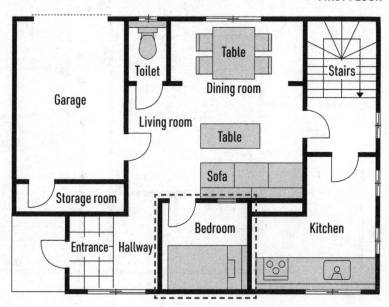

## DAYDREAM

KURIHARA: This house was once home to a couple and their only child. The child, for some unknown reason, was imprisoned in its bedroom. The couple occasionally invited guests to stay.

They would chat in the living room before serving dinner in the dining room. Perhaps the husband would pour a few too many drinks. The guest would drink up, enjoying the meal and generally getting into good spirits.

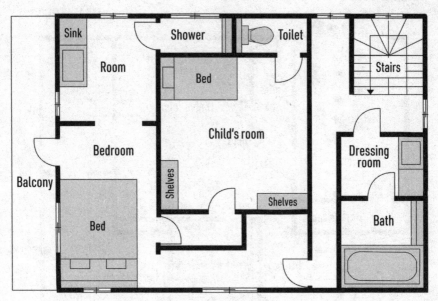

SECOND FLOOR

Sink

Room

Shower

Toilet

Stairs

Bed

Child's room

Bedroom

Shelves

Dressing room

Balcony

Bed

Shelves

Bath

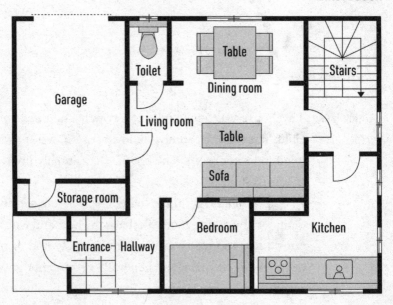

FIRST FLOOR

Garage

Toilet

Table

Dining room

Stairs

Living room

Table

Sofa

Storage room

Bedroom

Kitchen

Entrance

Hallway

Then, when the guest realized they'd had a bit too much, the missus would suggest, 'Why don't you stay the night? We've got a spare bedroom. We've even run a bath already. Go on!'

They would lead their unwitting guest to the windowless bathroom on the second floor.

When they were sure their guest was washing in the bathroom, they would send some kind of signal to the child's room. The child would climb down through the hole in their floor, crawl through the first-floor passage, and up into the bathroom. And then . . . stab the guest to death.

AUTHOR:     What?! Where on earth did that idea come from?

KURIHARA:   Well, like I said, it's just a little daydream of mine.

You have this guest, naked and defenceless, groggy with drink, completely unsuspecting. They can't put up a fight. Then the child creeps in and plunges a knife into them. Over and over. Blood stains the water. And the guest, uncomprehending to the very end, slips beneath the water and dies.

In other words, this house was built for murder.

AUTHOR:     You must be joking!

KURIHARA:   Sure, mostly. But . . . it's not out of the question.

Have you ever looked up 'unsolved murders' on the internet? There are loads of them out there, and plenty that rival the most frightening horror novel. Crimes that are twisted beyond imagination, happening in real life.

So, this? A couple who have a house built, then use their child to commit murders without getting their

31

own hands dirty? I wouldn't say it's impossible at all, personally.

AUTHOR: Well, all right, but . . . let's say you're right. Why would they do it?

KURIHARA: That is the question. . . . I doubt they'd have gone to such lengths just to kill one person. Clearly, they must have been killing people on a somewhat regular basis. And, if that's the case, the murders wouldn't have been carried out to satisfy a personal grudge. Maybe they were doing it on contract.

AUTHOR: Contract?

KURIHARA: There are plenty of sites advertising killers for hire. Part of the whole 'dark web' thing that was such a big deal in the news a while ago. Most of them are nothing more than scams, but I hear some are real. And some people will kill for as little as two or three hundred thousand yen. They might just be amateur hitmen, but as time moves on, their MOs get cleverer and more varied.

AUTHOR: So, you're saying this house is like a hired killer workshop?

KURIHARA: I'm just saying that's one way of thinking about it. Still, like I said, it's all just daydreaming on my part.

A couple of killers for hire using their child to murder people. It was pretty wild, even for a daydream.

KURIHARA: I've got one more daydream. You said earlier that they used the shelves to hide the secret passageway. Well, the child's room has another set, right?

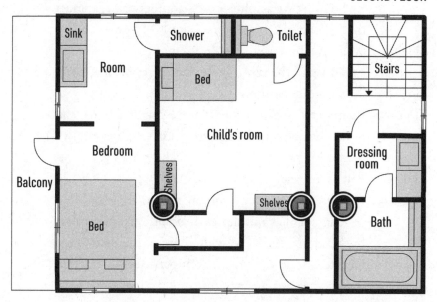

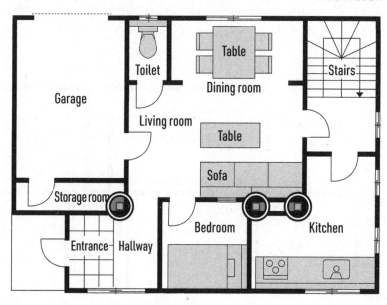

33

Couldn't we assume there's another passage under that second set?

AUTHOR: Well . . .

KURIHARA: And if that's the case, where does that hole lead to?

AUTHOR: To the storage room.

KURIHARA: Right. The storage room. So, we might say that this house has also been designed for easy disposal of bodies.

AUTHOR: You've lost me.

KURIHARA: Let's go back to what I was saying earlier.

The couple's murder is all done. But it's not like they can just leave the body there in the bath. They have to get rid of it without anyone seeing. So, they use the passage again—this time, to move the body. But the passage is too small for an adult to get through. So, the couple use a saw or something to cut the body into smaller pieces. Pieces just small enough to pass through the holes, and for a child to carry.

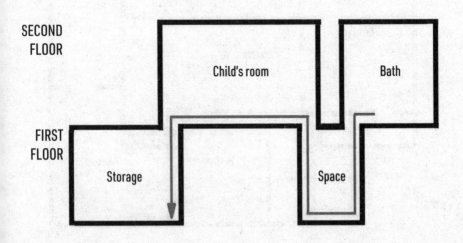

34

AUTHOR:    What?!

KURIHARA:  So, the couple drop the cut-up pieces through the hole. The child takes each piece up into their room and then drops it through the other hole. That's how they move the body from the bath into the storage room, which is next to the garage. So, they can easily pack the body into the trunk of their car and drive straight to some mountainside or forest to dispose of it.

*It was near a station, not far from forested hillsides.* That was one of the house's selling points.

KURIHARA:  The whole process can take place in rooms without windows. Meaning, they can do it all without worrying about being seen from outside. They can kill day or night, any day of the year. What do you think?

We were on Kurihara's turf here, so I wasn't prepared to challenge him. But there was one thing still bothering me. . . .

AUTHOR:    So, even supposing all this were true . . . why use such a convoluted method? If they wanted to kill someone without anyone seeing, couldn't they just close all the curtains in the house?

KURIHARA:  They could, sure. Usually, if you don't want people seeing what's going on in your house, that's what you'd do. Especially if you're, you know, murdering people. On the other hand, if you kept all the curtains open, no one would ever suspect you were killing people in there.

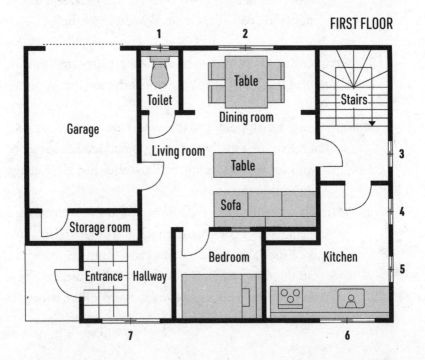

## SECOND FLOOR

8  9  10  11

Sink

Room

Shower

Toilet

16

Bed

Stairs

Child's room

12

Bedroom

Dressing room

Balcony

Shelves

Bath

Shelves

15

Bed

14  13

## FIRST FLOOR

1  2

Toilet

Table

Dining room

Stairs

Garage

Living room

3

Table

4

Sofa

Storage room

Bedroom

Kitchen

5

Entrance  Hallway

7  6

AUTHOR:   Ah, so it's a bit of psychological hocus pocus.

KURIHARA:   Right. Look at the floor plan again. This house has a lot of windows.

I counted them. There are sixteen altogether. It's almost like they're saying to the outside world, 'Go ahead, look at us. We have nothing to hide.' I'm sure they're actually a way of camouflaging the rooms that mustn't be seen.

AUTHOR:   You really think so?

KURIHARA:   Well, you know, this is all speculation. Don't take it too seriously, please.

I ended my call with Kurihara and sat mulling it over.

If I accepted Kurihara's story at face value, what should I do? Tell the police? Impossible. They'd never take it seriously enough to investigate.

The whole idea of 'a family of hired killers who built a murder house' was so bizarre that I'd be more concerned if they did in fact believe me. In fact, Kurihara might have concocted the whole story to tease me in the first place.

But right then, I had one important job to do: contact Yanaoka, who had asked for my advice on the house, and tell him what Kurihara and I had discussed. Setting aside the whole 'murder house' idea, he should know about the odd child's bedroom, at the very least.

# A GRISLY DISCOVERY

AUTHOR: Hello, good to talk to you again.

YANAOKA: Oh, hello there! I'm sorry for bothering you with that ridiculous request earlier.

AUTHOR: No, no, not at all. That's actually what I'm calling about. I was just talking about it to an acquaintance of mine, Kurihara. He's an architectural draughtsman. And . . . um . . . where should I start . . . ?

YANAOKA: Oh, well, actually . . . I really should have let you know. We decided not to buy the house, after all.

AUTHOR: You did? Why not?

YANAOKA: Well, I'm sure you already heard about, you know, the incident.

AUTHOR: What incident? Where?

YANAOKA: Didn't you watch the morning news? They found a chopped-up body in a thicket near that house.

AUTHOR: No way!

YANAOKA: It's kind of a bad omen, isn't it? So, today we let them know that we were no longer interested.

AUTHOR: I . . . I see.

YANAOKA: Honestly, though, we still feel a bit down about it. We really liked that house. It's barely lived in.

AUTHOR: Now that you mention it, when was it built?

YANAOKA: I think they said it was finished in spring of last year. So, just over a year ago, maybe?

So, the original owners put it on the market after living there for just a year. That seemed quite soon.

AUTHOR:    I was wondering, do you know where the previous owners are living now?

YANAOKA:    Sorry, I don't. And realtors can't share that kind of information. Client confidentiality, I suppose.

AUTHOR:    Right, of course.

YANAOKA:    I really am sorry for putting you to all this trouble! I owe you dinner sometime.

I hung up, then I looked up the news on my phone.

The headline came up right away: 'Corpse found in Tokyo'.

The body of a man was discovered in a thicket of trees in —— City, Tokyo, on September 8th. Officers from the —— Station of the Tokyo Metropolitan Police are currently seeking to identify the deceased.

According to a police spokesperson, the body was dismembered, with the head, arms and legs removed from the torso, but all the pieces were buried together. Only the left hand was missing.

The left hand was missing? What could that possibly mean?

I also wondered about the pieces being buried together. I would think, if someone had already gone to the effort of cutting a body into pieces, they'd surely scatter them in different places. That would slow down discovery and investigation, buying time for the murderer. But burying them all in the same place suggested the murderer had dismembered the corpse for another reason.

For example, to make it easier to carry through a narrow passage?

No, it couldn't be. That was all just a daydream. . . .

I decided to put it out of my mind and closed the news tab. Since Yanaoka had decided not to buy the house, it was no longer any concern of mine. I should just forget about it. I booted up my computer and got to work on an article with a looming deadline. But . . . I just couldn't concentrate.

That windowless child's room. Kurihara's explanation. The discovery of the body.

What was the truth behind that house?

## THE ARTICLE

Even a week later, I couldn't forget the house. When I was working, when I was eating, the whole time, that floor plan stayed in the corner of my mind. I opened up news sites on my phone again and again, checking for any progress on the case.

Then, one day, I mentioned the whole thing to my regular editor. 'Why don't you use the house as material for an article?' she suggested. 'You might even learn more about it from the readers.'

I was unsure. I was reluctant to publish baseless speculation about a real property.

But, at the same time, my curiosity was afire. I wanted to know more.

In the end, I decided to write the article but avoid including any specifics about the house's situation or appearance, to keep people from pinpointing its location. The information

I'd receive from readers may be less useful for it, but at least it could give me some fresh ideas or perspectives. Or so I hoped.

At the time, I never dreamt the article would end up revealing such a terrifying truth.

# CHAPTER TWO

# Another Warped Floor Plan

## AN UNEXPECTED EMAIL

After the article went live, several emails arrived from readers. Most were simply reactions to the story, but one stood out from the rest.

> I hope you forgive my presumption in contacting you. My name is Yuzuki Miyae.
>
> I saw the article you published the other day. I think I might know the house.
>
> If you don't mind, I'd like to discuss the matter with you further. I look forward to your response.
>
> Yuzuki Miyae<br>Telephone: 010-****-****

I was shocked. I looked back, but I hadn't given any hints as to the house's location. I didn't even think someone living in the neighbourhood could have worked it out. So, if she had recognized it, it must have been from the floor plan alone.

I suspected a prank, but she had included her name and phone number, and her tone had been so formal. Whatever was going on, I couldn't just let it go. I had to know more. So, I decided to get in touch.

After a bit of back and forth by email, I learnt the following:

- Yuzuki Miyae, the woman who had sent the email, was an office worker in Saitama Prefecture, next to Tokyo.
- She thought she knew something about that house.
- She wanted to share that knowledge with me, but, since it was a rather involved story, she wanted to meet and talk face to face.

To be honest, I was nervous about meeting her. I had no way of knowing what kind of person she was from her emails. What if she was someone directly connected to the house? A possible murder house!

But cowardice would never solve the mystery.

This could be my chance. I steeled myself and made an appointment to meet.

·　　·　　·

The next Saturday, I headed to the agreed-upon meeting place. It was a little café in a Tokyo business district. Miyae wasn't there when I arrived.

I ordered a coffee and waited. My palms were sweaty with nerves.

After a while, a woman entered. She had short hair and wore a beige business suit. She looked to be in her mid-twenties. She was carrying a large handbag. I recognized her as Miyae from the description she had sent.

I waved at her, and she spotted me. She came over, and our conversation started slowly.

MIYAE:     I'm sorry to have called you out here like this. It must
           have been a bother coming all this way.
AUTHOR:    Not at all. You had much further to come, after all. I'm
           glad we could meet. Will you have something?

She ordered an iced coffee. I was relieved to see—on first impres-
sion, at least—that she seemed perfectly normal. We chatted
idly for a while. She said she lived alone in a flat in Saitama and
worked as an office clerk.

When her iced coffee arrived, I decided to broach the main
topic.

AUTHOR:    So, what exactly did you mean when you wrote in your
           email, 'I think I might know the house'?
MIYAE:     Right. The truth is . . .

She sat quietly for a moment, gathering her thoughts. Then,
lowering her voice as if fearing to be overheard, she began.

MIYAE:     I think my husband might have been killed in that
           house.

## THE SECOND HOUSE

The words were a bolt from the blue. Miyae said, 'I'll start at the
beginning,' and told me her story.

MIYAE:     My husband, Kyoichi Miyae, left our house one
           September day three years ago, saying he was going

to visit a friend. He never returned. I should have asked in more detail where he was going, but I didn't. I don't know where he went. There were no witnesses, and he was never seen again. The police eventually gave up searching.

Then, a few months ago, a body was found on a mountainside in Saitama. DNA analysis confirmed it was my husband. But there was something odd about the remains. His left hand was missing.

AUTHOR: Really?!

The corpse found a few days ago had also been missing its left hand.

MIYAE: The police said it had been removed with some kind of bladed instrument.

But that's all we know. There didn't seem to be any clues pointing to who the murderer might be. Or what happened to Kyoichi. Or why they cut off his hand. I've been so desperate to find out the truth. I keep looking in newspapers and on the internet for any information that might somehow be connected to his murder. And that's how I happened to find your article.

You wrote that the left hand of that body was missing. Just like my husband's.

And then there's the idea of killing guests. I was thinking, what if it was that house he was going to visit the day he disappeared? I couldn't shake the feeling.

I know linking the two cases based on that one fact is a stretch. I really do. But I just can't believe they aren't connected.

AUTHOR: I see. They do share a few similarities. But that house was only built in spring of last year. You said your husband disappeared three years ago. So . . .

MIYAE: I know what you're going to say, that the house didn't even exist when my husband died.

AUTHOR: Yes.

MIYAE: There's something I'd like to show you to do with that.

Miyae retrieved a plastic document wallet from her bag, then removed a sheet of paper from it, placing it on the table. It was a floor plan.

AUTHOR: What is this?

MIYAE: It's the plan of a house. I think the owners of that other house might have lived here once.

AUTHOR: Once?

MIYAE: When I read in your article that the house in Tokyo was built last year, it got me wondering where the owners lived before that. If the story you came up with had any truth, then I thought they might have been using their child to kill even before then.

If that was the case, then their old house might also have had a child's room with no windows and a passage leading to the killing floor.

And if that house had ever gone up for sale, then I thought there might be a listing online somewhere. Including a floor plan. So, I decided to try to find it.

I began to comb through every property website I could find, looking for houses with similar floor plans to that one.

AUTHOR: You decided to search them all? I can't imagine how much information you must have sifted through.

MIYAE: I had some ideas to narrow it down. First, I thought the house must have been inside Saitama Prefecture.

AUTHOR: And why was that?

MIYAE: After my husband disappeared, I was cleaning out our room and found his long wallet in his desk. He used two wallets, each for different purposes.

One was his long wallet, where he kept his larger notes and credit cards. That's the one he took on longer business trips or when he was doing some major shopping. The other was a little pocket wallet with his commuter pass and smaller amounts of cash.

If my husband left his long wallet behind, then the house he was visiting couldn't have been far— somewhere in the prefecture, for sure. So, I focused my search on houses that went on the market within the last three years—between my husband's disappearance and the building of the Tokyo house—inside Saitama. And I paid particular attention to neighbourhoods near our own house.

Miyae looked down at the table.

AUTHOR: So, this floor plan is what you found?

MIYAE: Right. It was only about twenty minutes' walk from our home.

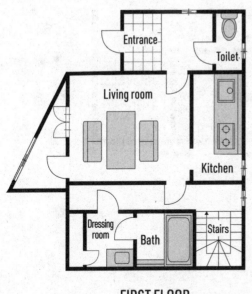
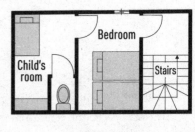

**FIRST FLOOR**   **SECOND FLOOR**

Somehow, it didn't sit right with me. It was too easy. Too lucky. I picked up the floor plan, half-believing, half-doubting.

It was a weirdly unbalanced design. Almost warped.

The front door leading into a hallway, a toilet, a living room and, next to that, a triangular room. I wondered what it could have been for.

I looked at the second-floor layout. And that's what sent a chill up my spine.

A windowless child's room. An en-suite toilet. Just like that other house.

AUTHOR:   You're right . . . they do look similar. Particularly the child's room.

MIYAE:   And not just that. Look at the first-floor bathroom.

51

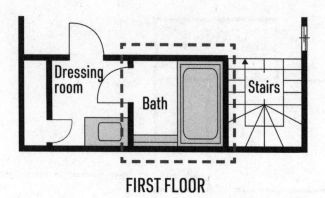

**FIRST FLOOR**

AUTHOR:    Oh. No windows.

MIYAE:     Right. And then there's that tiny space next to the dressing room. Doesn't that remind you of the 'mystery space' in the Tokyo house? It's even located directly below the child's room.

AUTHOR:    So, if there were a hole in the floor of the room leading down into that space . . .

MIYAE:     That would make it a passage connecting the child's room and the dressing room. And, see, there's a door leading to the dressing room from that little space.

So, the child would drop down through the hole into the space and hide there. The guest would get into the bath. When the time was right, the child would sneak out into the bathroom and kill the guest in the tub. The particulars might be different, but there was a route connecting the child's room to the bathroom, just like in the Tokyo house. Of course, that was assuming Kurihara's hypothesis was right. . . .

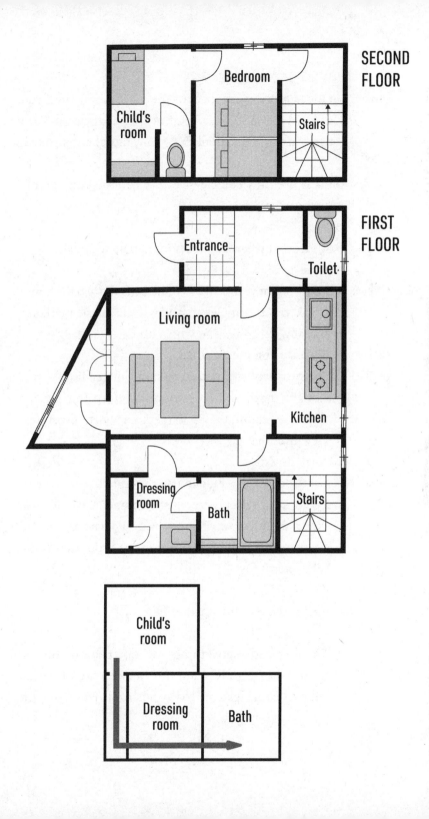

SECOND FLOOR

Bedroom

Child's room

Stairs

FIRST FLOOR

Entrance

Toilet

Living room

Kitchen

Dressing room

Bath

Stairs

Child's room

Dressing room

Bath

MIYAE:     What do you think?

AUTHOR:    Honestly, I was sceptical of the whole thing until you
           showed me this floor plan. But with all these similari-
           ties, I'm starting to think they really must be connected.

I didn't think it was all a coincidence. But had the same family
really lived in both houses?

AUTHOR:    So, around when did this house go up for sale?

MIYAE:     It was in March 2018.

AUTHOR:    Spring of last year . . . that's right around when the house
           in Tokyo was completed. And is it still on the market?

MIYAE:     Actually, it's gone. The whole house.

AUTHOR:    What do you mean, gone?

MIYAE:     The property site said it was 'no longer listed', so I
           thought they must have found a buyer. But when I
           asked the realtor, they told me it had burnt down just
           a few months ago.

AUTHOR:    Burnt down!

MIYAE:     Just the other day, I looked up the address and went to
           see for myself, but there's just an empty lot there now.
           I know there's so much more we could have discovered
           if it was still standing. I'm so curious about this room.
           What was it for?

Miyae pointed at the triangular room.

MIYAE:     There are so many things we don't know. But, if
           we could just understand this house better, I have a
           hunch it could lead me to my husband's murderer. Of

54

course, it's just a feeling—there's nothing to back up any of this.

AUTHOR: I see. For now, I'd like to show my draughtsman friend, Kurihara, this floor plan and get his opinion. Could I have a copy?

MIYAE: You can take this one. And here, take this as well. I don't know if it will be any help, but I printed out the full listing page from the property site.

AUTHOR: Thank you. I'll take them both.

MIYAE: I really am sorry for putting you to all this bother. Please give Mr Kurihara my thanks, as well.

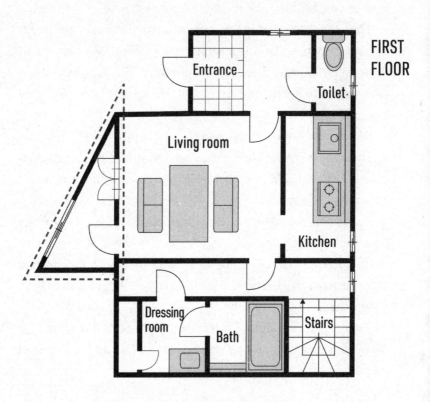

We left the café. The sun was blazing, and soon sweat poured down my face.

AUTHOR: Um. May I ask you something? I mean no disrespect, but did your husband ever have any trouble with anyone before he died?

MIYAE: Not that I know of. He was an honest man, and the idea that someone might have wanted him dead . . . it's hard to believe.

AUTHOR: I see. I hope they find the murderer soon.

MIYAE: Me, too. I just want them to tell me what actually happened.

Miyae and I parted at the station, and I boarded the train home. I sat and looked over the material she'd given me.

The —— Property site listed the address, the area of the building and garden, and its distance from the station. My eyes fell on the line 'House age: three years; built 2016'. So, they moved out after only two years. And the Tokyo house had been sold only one year after it was built, too.

Were these houses truly used to kill people?

I must be honest. When I first heard Kurihara's idea, and even as I wrote the article, I never actually bought into any of it. It was all just baseless speculation.

But after meeting Miyae, that speculation was starting to take on a feeling of reality.

Still, I wasn't convinced by Kurihara's theory about contract killers using a child. There surely had to be more to it than that. That's the feeling I had, anyway.

Then I had a thought. I took out my phone and searched for 'Kyoichi Miyae'. I found several hits for news articles. I opened one dated to July of that year:

The remains discovered on the 25th of last month in ——
City, Saitama Prefecture, have been identified as those of
Kyoichi Miyae, who went missing in 2016. Mr Miyae's body
was found with its left hand severed. . . .

The last phrase held me fast: '. . . with its left hand severed'. That
implied that nothing except the left hand had been cut off. So,
Kyoichi Miyae's corpse had not been cut into pieces.

I switched tabs and opened a news story about the body discovered in Tokyo. There was still no progress.

The left hands of both bodies were missing. However, one
body had been dismembered, and the other hadn't. Were the
murders truly by the same person?

## DIFFERENCES

After I got home, I compared the layout of the house I got from
Miyae and the one for the Tokyo house.

They had much in common. But there were also notable
differences.

For example, the Saitama house had no garage. Without a
garage, that house had no route to dispose of the body.

And then I noticed something else.

If they murdered someone in the Saitama house, the killers
wouldn't have needed to pass the body via the hidden passage
through the child's room. So, they would not have needed to cut
it into pieces. That must be why Kyoichi Miyae's body had been
intact. Well then, how had they transported the body out?

57

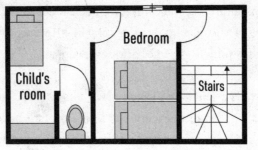

SECOND
FLOOR

Child's
room

Bedroom

Stairs

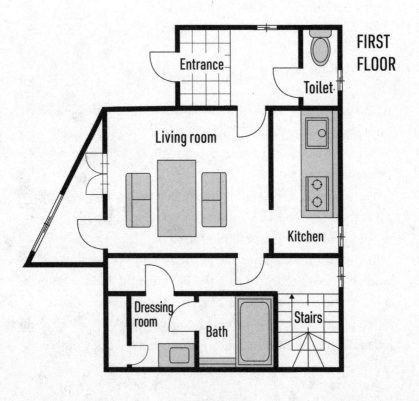

FIRST
FLOOR

Entrance

Toilet

Living room

Kitchen

Dressing
room

Bath

Stairs

SAITAMA

## SECOND FLOOR

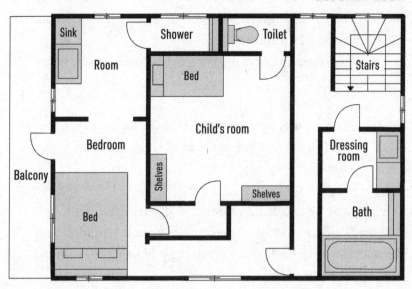

Sink

Room

Shower

Toilet

Stairs

Bed

Child's room

Dressing room

Bedroom

Shelves

Shelves

Bath

Balcony

Bed

## FIRST FLOOR

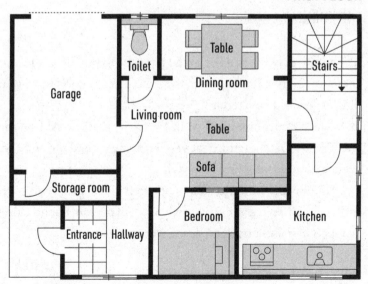

Toilet

Table

Dining room

Stairs

Garage

Living room

Table

Sofa

Storage room

Bedroom

Kitchen

Entrance

Hallway

# TOKYO

That evening, I emailed Kurihara a summary of the day's events and scans of the information I'd received on the Saitama house. Then I fell into an exhausted sleep.

I was awakened the next morning by the telephone ringing. It was Kurihara.

KURIHARA: Hello. Sorry for calling so early. I saw the email you sent last night. Can you meet up? I think I'm onto something.

When I pried for details, he admitted he'd been up all night studying the floor plans. I was amazed at his stamina. I couldn't drag the man out after he'd stayed up all night like that, so I agreed to go to his place.

## THE KURIHARA HOME

Kurihara was living in a flat in the Umegaoka neighbourhood of Setagaya, Tokyo. It was a rather squalid place, a good forty years old, but he said he liked it there.

It was twenty minutes' walk from the station. Although it was already October, the heat was lingering on and on, and I was drenched in sweat when I arrived.

I rang the bell, and Kurihara appeared in his usual T-shirt and shorts. It had been a while since we'd met in person, but his closely cropped hair and untamed beard were unchanged.

KURIHARA: Thanks for making the trip. It's blistering out, isn't it? Come in. Excuse the mess.

I stepped into his flat. His living room, about eight tatami mats in size, was littered with books, as usual. While many were architecture-related, the vast majority were mystery novels. More than seemed reasonable, actually.

AUTHOR: So many books. As always.

KURIHARA: That does seem to be where most of my money goes.

Kurihara talked on as he served some cold barley tea. After a quiet drink, he laid a sheet of paper on the table.

KURIHARA: This is a printout of the plan you emailed me last night. Talk about a surprise! The idea that there were two of these houses . . .

AUTHOR: I couldn't believe my eyes, either, when I first saw it.

KURIHARA: But isn't this Miyae something else? She was able to dig it up with almost no solid leads to go on.

AUTHOR: Finding her husband's killer must be quite the motivation. By the way, what about this room was she hung up on? The triangular room. Do you know what it's for?

KURIHARA: It is an odd one, isn't it? I'm not sure about the specifics, but there is one thing I can say for sure. This room was a later addition, after the house was built.

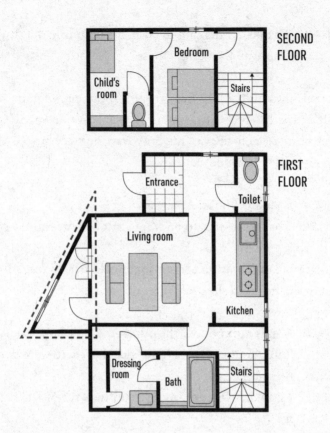

SECOND
FLOOR

Bedroom

Child's
room

Stairs

FIRST
FLOOR

Entrance

Toilet

Living room

Kitchen

Dressing
room

Bath

Stairs

## THE TRIANGULAR ROOM

AUTHOR:    It was? How can you be sure?

KURIHARA:  There's a window between the triangular room and
the living room. It's not all that unusual for houses
to have what they call 'interior windows', little open-
ings between rooms. But rarely, if ever, do you find
them in this double-leaf style. If opened all the way,
the panes would completely dominate the triangular room.

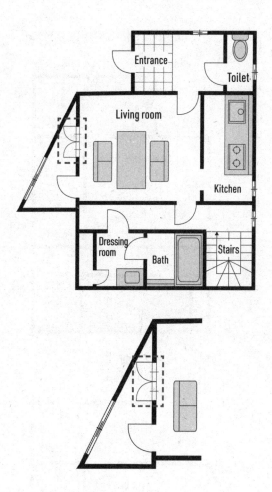

AUTHOR: I see what you mean. The windows would almost hit the wall on the other side.

KURIHARA: Yes, and the point of having big double-leaf windows is to let in light or air. But here, with the triangular room closing them off, they can't even fulfil their purpose. So, why have them at all?

My guess is that the window originally opened to the outside.

Kurihara covered the triangular room with his hand.

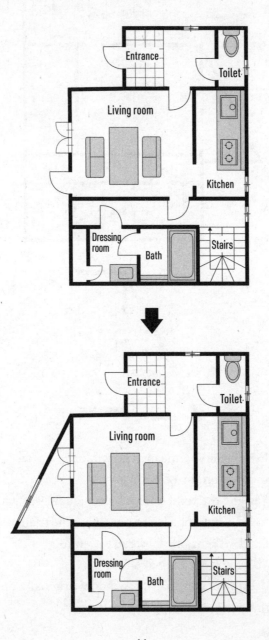

KURIHARA: When this house was first built, the triangular room
didn't exist. Look at this. Without those added walls,
the first floor of the house is conventional. You can see
outside through the living room window, with a door
opening into the garden.

AUTHOR: So, they added this triangular room over what was once
the garden. But why build it at all?

KURIHARA: I don't know, but I think I can guess as to why it was
triangular.

AUTHOR: Why's that?

Kurihara placed his laptop on the table. The screen showed an
aerial photo.

KURIHARA: I looked up the address on the net, from the materials
you sent. Let's see . . . here it is.

He was pointing his finger at a trapezoid-shaped empty lot,
enclosed by walls. The photo must have been taken after the
fire. Kurihara took out a notepad and traced the shape of the lot.

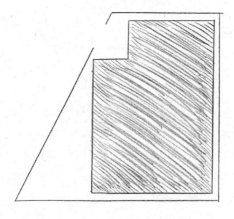

KURIHARA:   The house was originally built on this trapezoid-shaped lot, and the house itself was roughly rectangular, like this. They used the leftover triangular piece of land as a garden.

Then, for whatever reason, they needed to add another room. So, they made it triangular to fit the shape of the plot.

AUTHOR:   I see. They didn't have a lot of options there.

KURIHARA:   Maybe not. But there is one thing I don't get.

Kurihara added to his drawing.

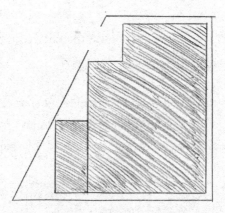

KURIHARA:   If they'd done something like this, they could have added a square room. The area wouldn't be all that different, and it would have been more convenient in general. Easier to build, too. So, why didn't they? One reason might be the garden itself.

66

If they'd built a square room, it would have left two small empty spaces. They'd have been hard to make much use of. But building a triangular room meant they left a decent amount of space at the bottom of the plot.

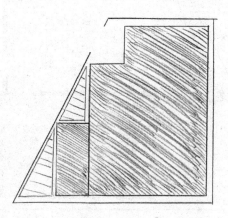

AUTHOR:     So, they probably went for the triangle to preserve some garden space.

KURIHARA:   That's what I initially thought. But the more I thought about it, the stranger it seemed. There's no door to the garden. The original house had a door letting out onto the garden from the living room. But adding the triangular room made it useless. And there are no doors onto the garden from any other room, either. So, it became inaccessible.

AUTHOR:     Hmm . . . couldn't they get there by squeezing along the outside wall of the triangular room from the front door?

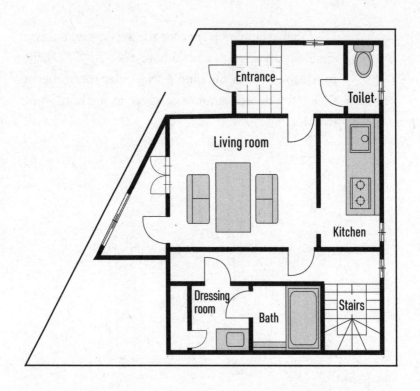

KURIHARA: No chance. I did some calculations based on the aerial photo and the data in those notes you sent me. The gap between the triangular room and the wall was only about twenty or thirty centimetres. That's not enough space for an adult to get through.

AUTHOR: So, there's actually no way to get into that space?

KURIHARA: That's right. I mean, I doubt they climbed up and walked along the top of the wall. So, I think we can safely say that, after adding the triangular room, they no longer had use of the garden space.

AUTHOR: Then why did they decide to leave it?

KURIHARA: They didn't decide to leave it. . . . They had to. They could not build a room over that area.

AUTHOR: What do you mean by that?

KURIHARA: When you build a structure, you have to drive long columns into the dirt to support the building—we call it 'pile driving'. I have a feeling that, for a very important reason, they could not drive piles in this space.

AUTHOR: And what was that important reason?

KURIHARA: Things that usually prevent pile driving are the soil being either too hard or too soft. But I doubt that the soil quality was that different so close to where they actually built the room. So, then, another possibility is that there's something under there. For example, a cellar.

AUTHOR: What?!


## THE BURIED ROOM

KURIHARA: Let's step back for a moment. This house doesn't have a garage, right?

Let's say that this house was used for murder. They couldn't move the body without a car. And without a garage, they would have had to park the car in front of the house and carry the body out to it. There would have been a real risk of somebody seeing them. I doubt anyone who went to the trouble of building a house just to kill people would ever have taken such a risk. So then, how did they get rid of the bodies?

I think they might have hidden them in the house itself.

69

AUTHOR: You mean they had some kind of dead body storage area?

KURIHARA: Right. But, where?

It would have needed to be a fairly large space,
sealed off so the smell couldn't get out, set apart from
the actual living space. And, of course, not visible from
the outside. There is no room in this house that meets
these requirements. In which case, one possibility is the
existence of an underground room.

Kurihara tapped the space next to the dressing room.

KURIHARA: Couldn't this space serve both as a passage and as an
entry to the underground room? The couple could
drag the body from the bath into this space, open the
trap door and store the corpse in the underground
room. And just like that, their body problem is taken
care of.

AUTHOR: But wouldn't the floor plans include a cellar, if there
were one?

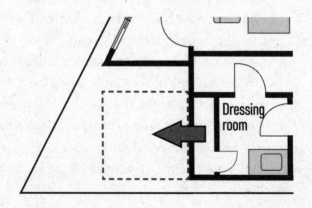

70

KURIHARA: This floor plan was taken from a property site. Which means it's one that the realtors had commissioned when the house went up for sale. The owners might well have sealed it off completely before then.

AUTHOR: So . . . there could still be bodies buried there?

KURIHARA: No, I don't think there's any chance of that. They'd have had no way of knowing if or when someone might go digging there after they sold the house. I imagine they hid the bodies somewhere else when they sealed off the cellar. They found Kyoichi Miyae's remains on a mountainside, right?

AUTHOR: That's right.


## CHANGES

KURIHARA: But that still leaves one problem with this triangular room. Why would they have it built, with all the risk it would bring?

AUTHOR: What risk?

KURIHARA: Adding a room to a house is a pretty big job. There would be builders going in and out for a while, and it would attract attention from the neighbours. For this family, that could be a matter of life and death.

So, what would have compelled them to add this room, considering all the risk involved?

Outside, the bells chimed for twelve o'clock.

KURIHARA: Oh, it's noon already. Shall we order something to eat?

71

We ordered some lunch to be delivered from a neighbourhood soba noodle shop. While we waited, I got Kurihara's input on something I'd been mulling over.

AUTHOR: I think I'm going to go and see this Tokyo house.

KURIHARA: Why's that?

AUTHOR: Well, the Saitama house has burnt down, but the Tokyo house is still up for sale. If I ask, the realtors will let me view it. If I could find some kind of evidence, some proof that people died there, we would finally know that it really was a murder house. And then we might actually be able to convince the police to take this off our hands and investigate properly.

KURIHARA: I think that might be difficult.

AUTHOR: You do?

KURIHARA: They would have had a professional inspection before the house went up for sale. If it cleared the inspection, at the very least there can't have been any visible evidence. Nothing obvious like traces of blood or anything. And they'd have sealed up the passage, I bet.

I mean, a forensics team might be able to turn up DNA from the victims or something, but you'll never spot anything just by taking a tour. Anyway, one thing I think we can do is clarify the biggest mystery of this floor plan here and now.

AUTHOR: You mean the triangular room?

KURIHARA: That, too, but what I'm really thinking about are the differences between the two houses.

Kurihara laid the two floor plans side by side.

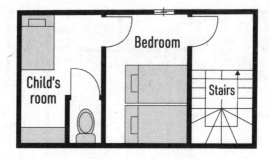

SECOND
FLOOR

Bedroom

Child's
room

Stairs

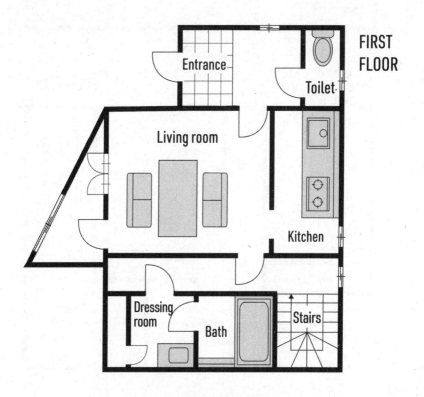

FIRST
FLOOR

Entrance

Toilet

Living room

Kitchen

Dressing
room

Bath

Stairs

SAITAMA

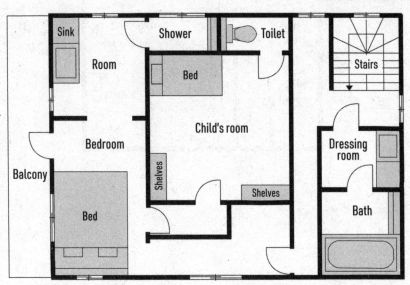

Sink

Room

Shower

Toilet

Bed

Child's room

Bedroom

Shelves

Shelves

Balcony

Bed

Dressing room

Bath

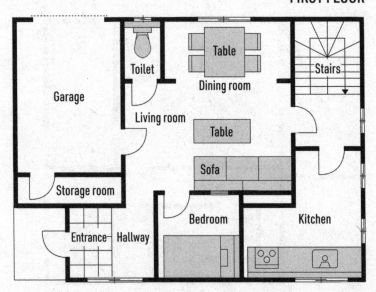

Stairs

Table

Toilet

Dining room

Garage

Living room

Table

Stairs

Sofa

Storage room

Bedroom

Kitchen

Entrance

Hallway

# TOKYO

KURIHARA: For example, look at the number of windows. In the Saitama house, there are very, very few. Meanwhile, the Tokyo house has so many that it's almost like they're inviting people to look in.

There's also the difference in the child's bedroom doors. The Tokyo house has vestibule-style double doors, while the Saitama house just has one. And next there's the couple's room. The Saitama house has two single beds. In other words, the mother and father slept in different beds. But in Tokyo, they slept together in a double. You don't really hear about couples whose relationships improve with a move, do you? Something else must have changed between them.

If the same people lived in these two houses, what caused those changes? If we can figure that out, I think we'll be one step closer to identifying the family.

AUTHOR: I see.

KURIHARA: In that respect, visiting the Tokyo house might not be such a bad idea. Even just seeing the exterior might give us a clue. Oh, and here's the soba. Let's eat.

We did so, and then I left Kurihara's flat. On the train home, I summed up our discussion in my notepad:

- The triangular room was added on for some unknown reason.
- It's possible that they had a cellar under the garden to store dead bodies.
- Differences from the Tokyo house: number of windows, doors on the child's bedroom, the couple's beds.

After I got home, I wrote these points out in an email to Miyae. A few hours later, I got this reply:

Thank you for your email.

I appreciate you keeping me updated.

I'm surprised you were able to figure out so much just from the floor plan. Please share my gratitude with Mr Kurihara.

I'm afraid I must be selfish once more and ask if you would meet me again. I would like to thank you in person, and there is also something else I wish to tell you. I can come to Tokyo, so, if you don't mind, let me know when you are free.

Yuzuki Miyae

## THE TOKYO HOUSE

The next Monday, I left early in the morning to visit the Tokyo house. Miyae and I were planning to meet at three in the afternoon. First, though, I had another matter to attend to.

The Tokyo house. What had initially set this whole investigation into motion. Like Kurihara had said, just a glance at the property might reveal something important.

It was a ten-minute walk from the nearest station. I found the house in a quiet residential neighbourhood.

White painted walls. Lush green garden. A totally ordinary sight. There was a 'For Sale' sign out in front. It was hard to imagine a murder happening in there. I stood and stared at the house. An odd feeling began to come over me.

76

Just then, someone spoke to me.

'If you're looking for the Katabuchi family, they've already moved.'

I turned around to find myself facing a woman in the neighbouring garden. She was around fifty, cradling a small dog, and looked as pleasant a person as you could hope to see.

WOMAN:    Are you a friend of the Katabuchis?
AUTHOR:   The people who lived here . . . they were called Katabuchi?
WOMAN:    That's right. The folks who lived here before.

So, now I knew their name. Katabuchi.

WOMAN:    Are you not a friend of theirs? What do you want with this house, then?

That threw me. I couldn't exactly admit that I had come to see a 'murder house'.

AUTHOR:   Umm . . . actually, I'm thinking of moving to this area and was walking around the neighbourhood to see if there were any houses up for sale.
WOMAN:    Oh, is that so? It's a nice, quiet place to live, you know.
AUTHOR:   It does seem lovely.
WOMAN:    And that's a nice house. Big and pretty. I can't for the life of me imagine why the Katabuchis would move out all of a sudden.
AUTHOR:   So, those . . . umm, Katabuchis. . . . What were they like?

WOMAN: A lovely family, just lovely. They got along so well. And the child was a darling.

AUTHOR: You saw their child?

WOMAN: I did. A little boy, he was. Hiroto, they called him. They said he'd just turned one when they moved in. He and his mummy were always out and about.

I was confused. If what she was saying were true, then we had got it wrong about the 'child prisoner'.

WOMAN: And then, one day, all of a sudden, they just up and left. So sad.

AUTHOR: All of a sudden, you say?

WOMAN: That's right. You'd think they'd have said something, us being neighbours and all. . . .

AUTHOR: They didn't even say goodbye?

WOMAN: Not a word! I think something must have happened.

AUTHOR: Hmm. Did you notice any changes before they moved out?

WOMAN: Let's see . . . oh, now that you mention it, my husband says he saw something odd over there.

AUTHOR: Oh, I'd love to hear about it, if you don't mind.

WOMAN: I don't, but . . . why are you so interested in the Kata-buchis, anyway?

AUTHOR: Oh, uh, just . . . you've just got me curious, I suppose.

WOMAN: Fair enough. Let's see . . . it was about three months before they moved, I guess. He got up for the necessary late at night. The window in our bathroom looks out onto the Katabuchi house. But he said, late as it was, there was a light on, and someone was standing in the window. See? That window right there.

The woman pointed at the window in the couple's bedroom on the second floor.

WOMAN:     He squinted, trying to see who it was. . . . He said it was a child he'd never seen before.

AUTHOR:    What?!

WOMAN:     He said it looked to be a boy, pale as a sheet, and maybe ten years old or so. There shouldn't have been any child like that next door, you know? We thought maybe some relative had come to visit. The next morning, we asked the mister over there. And he said we must be mistaken.

AUTHOR:    That is . . . odd.

WOMAN:     Anyway, I just hope, wherever they are, they're happy and healthy.

I thanked the woman and left. As I walked, an unpleasant feeling began to swell in my chest.

There were two children.

I rang up Kurihara and told him what I'd learnt. About Hiroto, the sudden move and the child standing in the window. He was silent for a moment, then spoke, his voice quiet:

'If . . . if there were two children, that would explain it all. Can you come over? Right away?'

I checked the time and saw it was only eleven. I had plenty of time before I was supposed to meet Miyae.

I headed for Kurihara's flat.

## TWO CHILDREN

Books still filled Kurihara's room. He'd spread the two floor plans out on his table.

AUTHOR: It really took me by surprise. There were two children!

KURIHARA: I never even considered the possibility myself. But thinking about it now, there being two kids solves everything nicely. First, though, let's establish a timeline.

The Saitama house was built in 2016. Two years later, in 2018, the family moved to the house in Tokyo. According to the neighbour, Hiroto had just turned one when they moved in. That would mean he was born in 2017. So, Hiroto was born while the Katabuchi family was living at the house in Saitama.

Before Hiroto's birth, there were three members of the Katabuchi family living in the Saitama house. The mother, father and the unnamed boy. Let's call him X.

The couple kept X confined in the second-floor child's bedroom.

And then, at some point, things changed for the family. Their second child, little Hiroto, was born. This triangular room was most likely built for him, don't you think?

AUTHOR: You're saying it's a nursery?

KURIHARA: I am. It's a little small, but I imagine a cot would fit just fine. It also has nice big windows to keep it bright and airy.

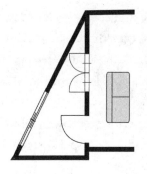

**2016** Saitama house completed
**2017** Hiroto born
**2018** Move to Tokyo

AUTHOR: But do you honestly believe a family that used their oldest son to murder people would care enough about their newborn to build a whole room for him?

KURIHARA: I do. From what the neighbour told you, the couple doted on Hiroto and took him out on walks. It's totally different from what X went through.

From that, what I surmise is that it's possible X wasn't their son by birth. Now, I think you mentioned before that a 'family of three' had lived in the Tokyo house. Who told you that?

AUTHOR: Yanaoka did, and he heard it from the realtors.

KURIHARA: Which would mean that the Katabuchis lied to the realtors. Because, of course, they're a family of four. But that lie would surely have been exposed when they submitted their family registration on signing the contract.

The fact that it wasn't exposed can only mean that X is not on the Katabuchi family register. They had an unregistered child. They might even have bought him. . . .

AUTHOR: You're talking about human trafficking.

81

KURIHARA:  Yes, maybe. At any rate, the couple never showed any affection at all for X. Yet, even murderous monsters can feel love for their own child. They showered Hiroto with affection. What a horrible double nature they displayed.

Naturally, people tend to care more for their own children than other peoples'. But this was beyond my grasp. I struggled to see any humanity in the Katabuchi couple.

KURIHARA:  Right, here's what I think.

    The couple were worried about how to raise Hiroto. They were in a house where murder was a regular occurrence. They didn't want to raise their darling son in such a hostile environment. If they could, they'd have built an entirely different home for him. But that was simply not possible.

82

So, as a compromise, they added this triangular room.

From the layout, this is the only room in the house that stands out. It is a bright, sunny room that stands in direct contrast to the rest of the gloomy murder house. And little Hiroto would grow up there, blissfully unaware of what was going on nearby.

AUTHOR: At the same time, X was confined to his room and forced to kill. If they really wanted Hiroto to be happy, they should have stopped killing people, instead of building a room.

KURIHARA: They might not have been able to quit, even if they wanted to.

AUTHOR: Why not?

KURIHARA: I've been thinking it over. About whether or not they were—or still are—voluntarily killing people. I think there's a possibility that someone else may be forcing them to do it.

AUTHOR: Some kind of ringleader, in other words.

KURIHARA: Right. If that's the case, their lives must be pure hell. Lives filled with terror and guilt. And for them, little Hiroto's birth must have been their only glimmer of hope. Maybe they felt that raising Hiroto in a happy home was a kind of salvation.

AUTHOR: Like they were living vicariously through him.

KURIHARA: Something like that, yeah. Thinking of things that way changes my reading of this other house.

Kurihara slid the Tokyo house floor plan to the centre of the table.

KURIHARA: In 2018, the family moved to Tokyo for some reason. They took that chance to build a new house. I think I mistook one thing about this house. I think the couple meticulously planned it out so they could raise their newborn child in peace and continue the murders at the same time.

## TWO FACES

KURIHARA: This house has two faces. I suppose you could call them light and dark.

The light face shows itself in those rooms where there are lots of windows: the living room, kitchen and bedrooms. They can be seen from outside, and there is nothing there to hide. Those rooms were expressly built for Hiroto. The couple used those rooms to play the ideal family as they raised him.

But, at the same time, the house has a darker face too. The child's bedroom, bathroom and the mysterious dead space. They are places where no sunlight reaches, and where the couple use X to commit murder. And the boundary where light meets dark is the double-door vestibule connecting the bedroom and the child's room.

When I first saw this layout, I thought those heavy double doors were installed to ensure that the child could never escape. But the Saitama house doesn't have the same setup. That struck me as odd. Now, though, I think I understand.

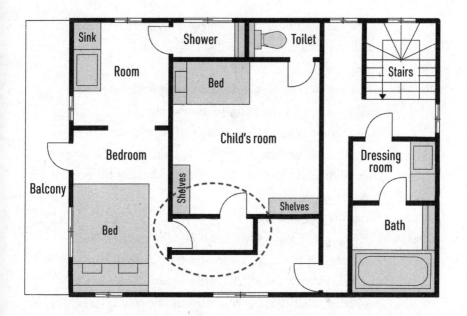

Those doors were there to make sure X and Hiroto never met.

So, for example, when the parents took a meal to X, if there were only one door to the room, there'd be a chance that X might see Hiroto. But with two doors, there was no chance of that happening.

AUTHOR: You think they wanted to keep X from knowing that Hiroto even existed?

KURIHARA: Well, living in the same house, I imagine it'd be impossible to keep him from noticing entirely. He'd surely have heard Hiroto crying or whatever. But they couldn't know how X would react if he actually saw Hiroto face to face. They might even have been afraid that he would be so jealous of Hiroto living such a different life that he would want to harm the baby. Even

85

as they kept X under tight control, they were probably terrified of him.

AUTHOR: I see.

KURIHARA: So, if we accept this new theory, that explains the double doors. In the Saitama house, the couple slept in separate single beds. But, in the Tokyo house, there was one double bed. How do we explain this difference? I'll just jump to my conclusion: that double bed was not for the couple.

AUTHOR: What do you mean?

KURIHARA: I think that bed was for Hiroto and his mother. With a bed in that position, she could take care of Hiroto and keep watch over the child's room. If the worst happened, and X got out of his room, she could protect Hiroto.

The reason the dressing room is completely open to the bedroom was also so she could keep an eye on the bedroom while she was in there.

AUTHOR: So, what was the father doing during that time?

KURIHARA: I'd imagine he was keeping watch over the whole house.

Remember the bedroom on the first floor? I do still think it was used for guests, but I imagine that, most of the time, the father slept there. The family regularly killed people. That could also mean their own lives were sometimes in danger. I'm thinking that the father must have seen his role as defender of the castle, to keep his wife and son from harm, so he slept down on the first floor to be close to the entrance.

86

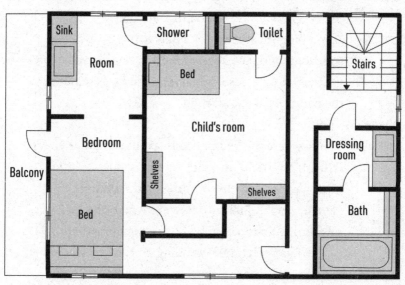

## SECOND FLOOR

Sink

Room

Shower

Toilet

Stairs

Bed

Child's room

Dressing room

Bedroom

Shelves

Shelves

Bath

Balcony

Bed

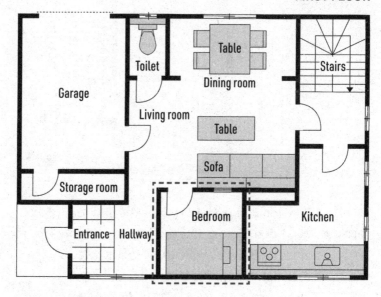

## FIRST FLOOR

Table

Dining room

Toilet

Stairs

Garage

Living room

Table

Sofa

Storage room

Bedroom

Kitchen

Entrance

Hallway

AUTHOR:    So, if X was kept in his room all the time, how could the neighbour have seen him that night?

KURIHARA:  Something must have just gone wrong that day, or at least something unexpected must have occurred. Now, the neighbour's husband said the child was standing in the bedroom window, right?

AUTHOR:    Right!

KURIHARA:  That's where the bed is. If this layout is right, then it's difficult to 'stand' in front of the window. I think X must have actually been sitting on the bed.

           The neighbour, not knowing where the bed was, saw him and just assumed he was standing there.

           I wonder what he was doing on the bed where his mother and Hiroto slept?

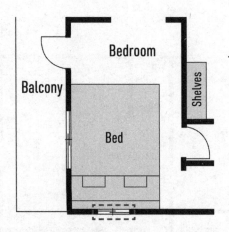

AUTHOR:    You don't think he hurt them, do you?

KURIHARA:  . . . I don't know. But the family did move out soon after. I think it's highly likely that whatever happened that night had something to do with it.

# SECRETS

KURIHARA: How are you for time, by the way? You had plans after this, right?

AUTHOR: Yes. I'm meeting Mrs Miyae at three.

KURIHARA: Ah, Mrs Miyae, is it? So, I have to be honest about something. I've been looking into the Kyoichi Miyae murder this past week.

Kurihara bent down to pick up a notebook from the floor and started to leaf through it.

KURIHARA: As I was reading through the newspaper and web articles from the time, I actually gathered a lot of information. But one thing I learnt has been bothering me quite a bit.
Kyoichi Miyae was not married.

AUTHOR: He wasn't?!

KURIHARA: No. Look at this.

Kurihara held out the notebook. It was a scrapbook filled with all kinds of article printouts. He pointed at one, apparently from the local newspaper. One underlined section read: 'The deceased, Kyoichi Miyae, was a bachelor. . . .'

AUTHOR: But . . . I'm certain that she called him her husband.

KURIHARA: I suppose it's possible they had some kind of common-law marriage, or maybe they were engaged. Regardless, I would be wary of trusting her too much.

.    .    .

I left his place at one-thirty. Kurihara saw me off, saying, 'Let me know if anything happens.' I walked towards the station.

Sweat poured down my face. It wasn't just the heat. Thoughts raced through my head, one after the other.

Who really was this person I was heading out to meet, the person that called herself 'Yuzuki Miyae'? Why had she contacted me? What connections did she have with that house? And what was this 'something else' she wanted to tell me?

I arrived at the station just as the express train was coming in. I figured I might as well go ahead and meet her.

I arrived at the café at a quarter to three, still unsure what to think. I stood outside the door, my heart pounding. I couldn't help it. I was anxious. I kept thinking I still had time to leave. To turn back. But if I did, I'd never learn the truth.

I made up my mind and opened the door.

Inside, I found her sitting at a table in the back. She noticed me, stood up and bowed a little. I reached the table, nearly quaking with nerves.

After a simple greeting, I intentionally avoided touching on my fears and explained Kurihara's analysis: the fact that there were two children; the couple's doting on Hiroto; the true meaning of the layouts. I tried to gauge her reaction as I spoke.

At first, she nodded and interjected normally as she listened, but as I went on, I saw her brow furrow. When I reached the point where the family suddenly left the Tokyo house, she abruptly blurted out, 'Excuse me,' and rose to her feet as if to escape.

Something about her story was off. I had even sensed it at our first meeting.

The feeling Miyae exhibited towards that family was not the anger of a victim towards perpetrators.

And then there was the oddness of what she'd said when we parted: *I just want them to tell me what actually happened.*

After a while, she returned to the table.

She had calmed down, but her eyes were red and puffy. It looked like she'd been crying.

AUTHOR:   Are you all right?

MIYAE:   I'm sorry about that.

AUTHOR:   Umm . . . I hope you'll forgive me for being so blunt, but . . . what is your true connection to Kyoichi Miyae? I read an article about his murder, and it said he wasn't married.

She sat silently for a moment, then gave a small sigh, as if in resignation.

MIYAE:   So, you found out. I'm so sorry for lying to you.

AUTHOR:   So, then, it was right?

MIYAE:   Yes. Kyoichi Miyae was not my husband.

My name is . . . Yuzuki Katabuchi. My sister, Ayano Katabuchi, lived in that house.

## SISTERS

I couldn't wrap my head around it. The woman sitting in front of me was part of the same family?

Starting off with a curt 'This will be a long story', she began telling me all that had happened to her.

.    .    .

I was born in Saitama Prefecture in 1995. My father was an office worker, and my mother worked part-time. We were not a wealthy family, but we had a stable life and a happy home.

My sister was two years older.

Her name was Ayano. She was kind and beautiful. I was proud of her. She spoiled me, and I loved her.

But during the summer when I was ten years old, my sister suddenly vanished. One morning I woke up and she was no longer in the room next to mine. In fact, her bed, her clothes, her desk . . . everything of hers was gone. I was surprised, of course. I asked my mother what had happened, and all she would say was, 'From this day forward, your sister is no longer part of our family.' I could get nothing else out of her.

I knew it was strange. A child can't just suddenly become part of some other family. Even as young as I was then, I knew that's not something that happens.

But my mother and father only grew upset when I brought up the subject, and at the time, I had neither the knowledge nor the ability to look for her on my own. All I could do was accept it.

Even so, not a single day passed where I did not think about my sister. Every night, I lay in bed and cried because I missed her. I felt that if I could hold on to the hope that someday she would come back to me, my pain would ease, and I could go on. But even that was too naive.

After my sister vanished, my family fell apart. My father suddenly quit his job, shut himself away in his room and took to drinking. In 2007, he crashed his car while drunk and died.

After that, my mother married a man named Kiyotsugu. He was such an overbearing sort that I could never seem to get along with him.

At the time I was in my rebellious phase, angsty and quick-tempered. I was partly to blame, but my relationship with my mother started to deteriorate. I left home as soon as I graduated secondary school.

A friend from school helped me get a job at a company in Saitama. I rented a flat near my office and started life on my own.

Things settled down as I entered my twenties, and I started thinking less and less about my family. I suppose you could say that I tried not to think about them. There were too many unhappy memories there.

And then, in October 2016, I received a letter.

It was from Ayano.

I hadn't heard from her in so long, I was truly shocked. Since there was no other way for her to know my address, I assumed my mother had given it to her.

The letter, in her same old handwriting, was filled with love and sentiments like, 'I was so sad I couldn't see you,' 'I'm worried about you, Yuzuki,' and 'I hope we can meet some day.'

I was just so glad that my sister was alive and well.

I wanted to write an answer right away, but there was no return address. The letter did have a number, though, so I rang it.

My sister's voice on the other end of the phone had matured but bore the same kindness, and slightly nasal tone, that I remembered. I was overjoyed. We ended up talking for over an hour that day.

I learnt that she had recently married and was living in Saitama, as well.

Her husband's name was Keita, and he had taken her name when they married. And so, even married, she remained Ayano Katabuchi. She told me that she wanted to invite me over some-day, but that things were difficult for the time being.

We talked about all kinds of other things, too. Our childhood, friends we used to have, what we were into now.

Everything, anything but that day when she suddenly disappeared from our lives. I asked time and again, but she wouldn't tell me what had happened. And so, I still don't know where she'd been or what she had been doing all that time.

After that, we talked frequently.

What I really wanted was to meet and talk in person, but she had her own family to take care of, and I think there was something about her situation that she didn't want to talk about. So, I didn't push it. And anyway, things were already far, far better than before, when I had no contact at all.

But then one day, when she suddenly said she'd just had a baby, I honestly felt shut out. She hadn't even told me she was pregnant.

I suppose she was busy with her child, because there was no word from her for a while. I missed her, but I was also glad to think of her living happily with her family.

I finally heard from her again in May of this year.

I was surprised to learn that her family had moved to Tokyo. I had another shock when she invited me to their new house.

When I saw my sister for the first time in thirteen years, she had transformed into a lovely, maternal figure, though I could still see the shape of her childhood face. Her husband, Keita, seemed like a kind man, and little Hiroto was adorable. He looked just like his mother. They seemed like a perfect family.

But when I look back on it now, there were some odd things about the visit.

They told me that the stairs were being repaired, so I couldn't go up to the second floor. Even then, I thought it was strange that a newly built house already needed repairs.

And then . . . I'm not sure how to put it, but she and her husband always seemed afraid, or preoccupied about something. Now, I regret so much that I ignored all those little signs.

I lost contact with my sister again two months after I visited their Tokyo home.

I called her again and again, but she never answered. My texts went unread. I grew so worried that I went over to their house to look for her. It was empty. I asked around and learnt the family had suddenly moved out a few weeks before.

I was getting the feeling that my sister must have been struggling under some enormous stress the whole time. I finally realized how strange things had been since she got back in touch. How we couldn't meet when she was living so much closer, in Saitama. How there would be occasional long lulls in her calls and letters. And then this sudden move . . . something was very wrong. I couldn't just let it go.

The first thing I did was go and see my mother, though we had been estranged for years. I thought she might have an idea where Ayano was, but Mother is simply too stubborn. She wouldn't say a word. She wouldn't even let me in her home.

I also talked to the police, but moving house is no crime, so they turned me away. The realtors wouldn't tell me anything either, out of privacy concerns.

At which point, my last hope was the house in Saitama where they had lived before. I thought perhaps they had moved back for some reason. Honestly, I knew the chances were slim, but there was nothing else to go on.

I went back to the very first letter she had sent and used it to start searching for the house.

It didn't have a return address, but the postmark showed the post office where it was sent from. I reasoned that their house must be nearby. Ayano had mentioned that they had put their old house up for sale when we met in Tokyo. When I looked online, I found only one house in the area that had been put on the market during that time. I immediately jotted down the address and hurried over. All that was left was an empty lot.

It was at this point, with no more clues, at a complete dead end, that I happened across your article.

When I saw that floor plan, my heart stopped. It was my sister's house, without a doubt.

And then, there was that line at the end: *The corpse's left hand was nowhere to be found.* I felt like I had come across something similar before, then it clicked: it was the Kyoichi Miyae case. I'd only read about it the one time online, but the severed left hand was so disturbing that the story stuck with me.

When I checked again, I found that Mr Miyae had lived near my sister's house. A terrible suspicion began to form in my mind.

What if the story in your article was all true?

Then it occurred to me that if I could get the person who had written the article to look at the Saitama house's floor plan, they might be able to catch something I hadn't. That's why I got in touch with you.

I was worried that you would be too wary to meet me if I told you it was my sister's house. But if I claimed I had no connection to the place, you might not take me seriously. So, I pretended I was Kyoichi Miyae's wife.

I feel terrible for lying to you. I'm so sorry.

.     .     .

Her voice trembled as she apologized profusely.

AUTHOR: Please, it's all right, Ms . . . Katabuchi. I'm sorry too. I wrote the article out of simple curiosity, but it's clearly a very serious matter for you. If there's anything I can do to help, please just ask.

KATABUCHI: Thank you.


## THE SIGN

AUTHOR: But, from what you've just told me, I get the sense that this whole thing began with your sister's first disappearance, when you were ten. When a child disappears, it's usually because they were kidnapped or ran away. So, it's strange that your parents seemed to just accept it.

KATABUCHI: Yes, I know.

AUTHOR: Before she disappeared, did anything unusual happen, or was there any kind of sign that something was coming? Any changes in your family life, perhaps?

KATABUCHI: Well, I don't know if it's connected, but about a week before, my family had gone to stay at my grandparents' house. While we were there . . .

AUTHOR: Something happened?

KATABUCHI: Yes . . . one of our cousins died in an accident. But I have to be honest. I can't help but feel there was something suspicious about that too. In fact . . .

Katabuchi fell silent as a waiter came to clear away our empty cups.

97

My phone buzzed in my pocket. I saw I had a text from Kurihara: *Are you all right? Tell me all about it when you're done.*

A thought suddenly occurred to me.

AUTHOR: Hey, if you don't mind, would you be open to meeting a friend of mine, Kurihara? If you told him your story, he might provide some useful insights.

KATABUCHI: If it's no trouble for your friend, I'd be very happy to.

.     .     .

We stepped out of the café, and I called Kurihara. He eagerly agreed to meet, but added, *There's no way I can invite a woman to this pigsty.* He suggested an alternative venue, and we headed that way.

## WORKSPACE

We were to rendezvous at a building in front of Shimokitazawa Station. The sign out front read: 'Workspaces for Rent'.

A few minutes after we arrived, Kurihara came running up in his usual outfit. We did the greetings and introductions, and I could sense that Kurihara was a bit wary of Katabuchi. He still didn't know why she'd lied to me, so I understood his caution. That was probably the real reason he hadn't invited her to his place.

We registered and paid, then went up to the fourth floor to our rented conference room, where we sat around the table.

To begin with, I brought Kurihara up to date on everything

that Katabuchi had told me so far, while she chipped in with details as necessary. Kurihara took notes as he listened.

KURIHARA: I see. So, that's what was going on.

KATABUCHI: I do apologize for deceiving you both.

KURIHARA: Not at all. But I have to say, I'm a bit relieved. So, it's Ms Katabuchi, not Mrs Miyae, right?

KATABUCHI: Yes.

KURIHARA: Right, well, perhaps you could continue with your story now. What happened at your grandparents' house?

KATABUCHI: Yes, of course.

| | |
|---|---|
| **2006** | Cousin dies in accident (?) at grandparents' house |
| **2007** | Father dies in car accident |
| | Mother remarries |
| **2014** | Yuzuki moves out |
| **2016** | Yuzuki receives letter from Ayano |
| **2017** | Ayano gives birth to Hiroto |
| **2018** | Ayano's family moves to Tokyo |
| **2019** | Yuzuki visits Ayano's house |
| | Ayano's family disappears |

# CHAPTER THREE

## Drawn from Memory

# THE HOUSE OF THE ALTAR

KATABUCHI:  It was August 2006. We had gone to stay with my father's family in —— Prefecture (details redacted for privacy reasons). It was an old house built on a large plot of land cleared out of the woods on a mountainside. I don't think there were many other people living around there, just a few bed and breakfasts.

We used to visit every year during the summer holidays, but I never really liked going. It was just such a creepy old house. It's hard to put into words. Here, look at this floor plan.

Katabuchi opened her handbag and took out a piece of paper. It was a floor plan drawn in pencil.

AUTHOR:  Did you draw this yourself?

KATABUCHI:  I did. I looked up how to do it on the internet. I sketched what I could from my childhood memories. I could only guess at the size of the rooms, and I'm not really used to drawing, so please forgive the crudeness.

Katabuchi seemed quite embarrassed. Kurihara took the piece of paper and looked it over closely.

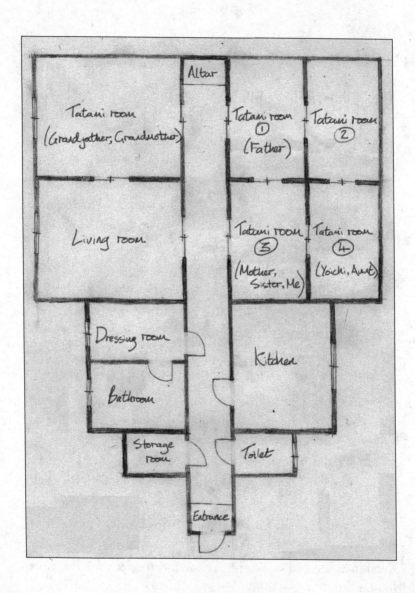

KURIHARA: Not at all. This is quite well done. You must remember the place very clearly.

KATABUCHI: I wouldn't say I generally have a good memory, but the house's layout was so strange, it's hard to forget it.

It was, indeed, a peculiar design. The house consisted of two symmetric halves, divided evenly by a long corridor. This symmetry was intentional, something we would only later discover. As we all peered at the drawing, Katabuchi began to describe the interior, as if digging up long-buried memories.

KATABUCHI: When you stepped through the front door, a long, dim hallway stretched out before you. At the far end you could just make out a large Buddhist altar. As you walked down the hall, on your left you'd find a storeroom, then a bathroom and dressing room, and finally the tatami mat rooms. Across the hall, you'd first pass a toilet, then a kitchen and, at the far end—mirroring the left half—tatami mat-floored rooms.

The first tatami room on the left was the living room, where everyone gathered and had meals. Beyond that, the room where my grandfather Shigeharu and grandmother Fumino slept, and where they usually spent most of their day.

Across the hall, an equivalent space was divided into four rooms, each about six tatami mats in size. I added numbers to the rooms to make it easier to remember which was which.

My father stayed in ①, while my sister, mother and I

stayed in ③. ② was always empty, and ④ was my Aunt
Misaki and her son Yoichi's room.

AUTHOR: Yoichi . . . Is that by any chance the cousin that you said
died in an accident?

KATABUCHI: That's right. He was seven when he died, three years
younger than me.

In checking the room assignments, I noticed that Yoichi's father
was conspicuously absent.

AUTHOR: What about his dad?

KATABUCHI: He had died of a heart attack about six months before.
His name was Kimihiko. He was the family's oldest
son. He and Aunt Misaki lived in the house after they
married, to look after my grandparents. But Kimihiko
always had a weak heart. It was tragic, him dying just
before his second child was born.

AUTHOR: A second?

KATABUCHI: That's right. Aunt Misaki was heavily pregnant when
all this happened, and the baby was due any time.

AUTHOR: A parting gift from Kimihiko, in a way.

KATABUCHI: Yes. I think Aunt Misaki had a terrible time of it, her
husband passing away when she was pregnant. And
then, what happened to Yoichi . . .

First the father, and six months later the firstborn son. It might
have been simple coincidence, but it had the feeling of fate
about it.

Then, Kurihara reached out and pointed at something on
the plan.

106

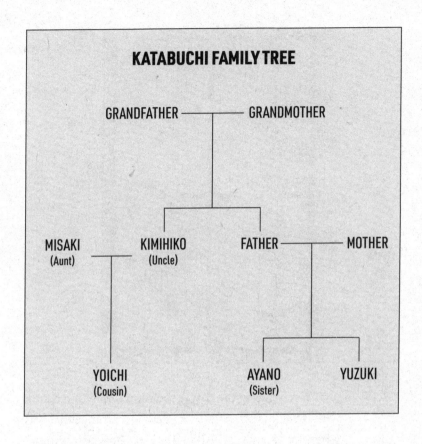

**KATABUCHI FAMILY TREE**

GRANDFATHER ——————— GRANDMOTHER

MISAKI (Aunt) ——— KIMIHIKO (Uncle)    FATHER ——— MOTHER

YOICHI (Cousin)    AYANO (Sister)    YUZUKI

KURIHARA: Ms Katabuchi, did Yoichi's room not have any windows?

AUTHOR: What?

I looked and saw that he was right. There was no window in room ④. More than that . . .

AUTHOR: Did none of the tatami rooms on the right side have windows?

KATABUCHI: That's right. I realized that as I was drawing the floor

107

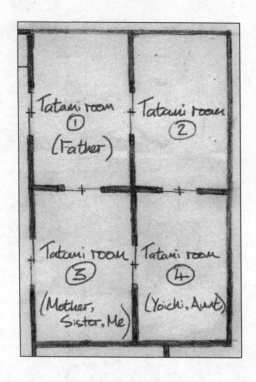

Tatami room ① (Father)

Tatami room ②

Tatami room ③ (Mother, Sister, Me)

Tatami room ④ (Yoichi, Aunt)

plan. Even during the day, those rooms were pitch dark with the lights off. I never noticed how strange that was when I was a child. It had kind of slipped my mind, honestly.

KURIHARA: Rooms with no windows. I can't help but think of the other two houses.

KATABUCHI: Me too. But, no matter how hard I try, I can't recall anything suspicious apart from that. No secret passages, no sealed spaces and, of course, never a hint that someone was locked away. But . . .

KURIHARA: What?

KATABUCHI: There was one set of fusuma sliding doors that wouldn't open.

108

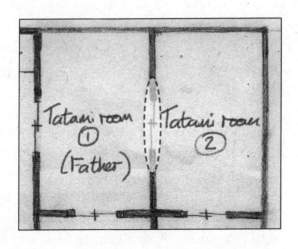

She pointed at the wall between rooms ① and ②.

KATABUCHI: These ones here. They would never open, no matter how hard we pulled. I thought they must be locked, but there was no keyhole.

AUTHOR: And all the others?

KATABUCHI: They all slid open and closed like normal.

AUTHOR: So, there weren't any inaccessible rooms?

KATABUCHI: No. Only, to get into room ②, you had to go around through ③ and ④, which was kind of a pain, so no one ever stayed in room ②.

KURIHARA: You said 'ever'. So, the doors had been stuck shut for quite a while?

KATABUCHI: Yes, I think so. But, well, the house was really old, so I couldn't tell you how long.

AUTHOR: Could you tell us when it was built?

KATABUCHI: I heard in the early Showa period, so in the 1920s or thereabouts.

AUTHOR:    It's seen a lot of history, then.

KATABUCHI: It has. In fact, this house was actually once part of a
           larger estate.

AUTHOR:    An estate?

After warning us that it would be a bit of a tangent, Katabuchi
recounted how the house was built.

KATABUCHI: I heard this story from my grandfather. Before the war,
           the Katabuchi family had earnt a fortune through all
           sorts of businesses. At its height, the family was wealthy
           enough to maintain a large estate with lots of servants.

           But, as the story goes, after a couple of generations,
           one day the head of the family handed control of his
           business operations to someone else and moved into
           an outbuilding in a distant corner of the estate. He cut
           himself off from the world, and from that point, the
           main manor fell into disrepair. Eventually, everything
           but the surviving outbuilding was demolished.

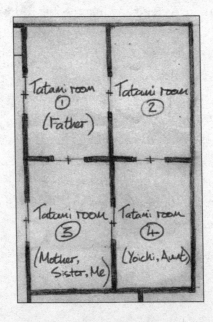

Over the years, the Katabuchi descendants scraped by on what little remained of the family fortune, expanding that sole remaining building.

AUTHOR: And that is this house?

KATABUCHI: That's right. I understood from family talk that the head of the family who first moved into the house had got involved with some strange religious cult, whose followers preached the sanctity of symmetry.

KURIHARA: But something must have happened, to make him shut himself away and devote his life to religion like that.

KATABUCHI: Well, Grandfather said that his wife died very young, and the loss nearly broke him. I think the house might have been built in her memory, actually.

You see this big Buddhist altar at the back? It was dedicated to her. It took up the full width of the corridor. Not a gap between it and the walls. I don't know if the house was built to fit the altar, or vice versa, but there was always a sense that the whole structure itself was a kind of Buddhist chapel.

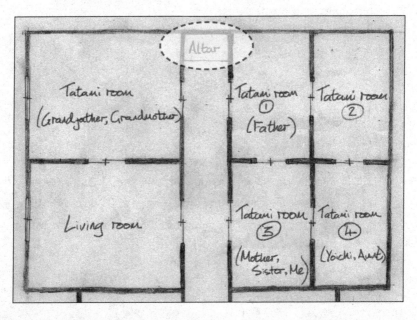

A giant Buddhist chapel . . . from the plan she'd drawn, it certainly did seem as if the altar was enthroned in the very centre of the house, like it ruled over the whole place.

KATABUCHI: One reason I didn't like going to my grandparents' house was that altar. It really was creepy. The way it loomed over me, and it had this weird black lustre to it. To me, it was the only truly strange thing in the whole house. Grandfather's legs were bad, so he spent most of his time in bed. Yet every morning, without fail, he would get up and clean the altar. One time, he asked me to help him. It's the only time I ever saw inside.

It had double doors that swung outward. Inside, there were things I'd never seen before, ritual items like bells and incense burners, and a big painting of a strange mandala pattern. I remember it all made me feel uncomfortable in ways I can't describe. The truth is . . .

Katabuchi broke off. After a few seconds of silence passed, she started again, in a hushed tone.

KATABUCHI: The truth is, Yoichi died in front of that altar.

## YOICHI'S DEATH

AUTHOR: That's where his body was found?
KATABUCHI: Yes. It was the third day of our stay. I think it was around five in the morning, actually. Everyone woke up to Aunt Misaki's screaming. We stepped out into

112

the corridor, and Yoichi was lying face up on the floor in front of the altar. His face was paper white, and his head was covered in black blotches of clotted blood. His body was ice-cold to the touch. I knew immediately: Yoichi was gone.

After that, their family doctor came and pronounced him dead. I can still see Aunt Misaki collapsed beside him, weeping and crying out, 'If only I'd noticed sooner!'

AUTHOR: From what you saw, it sounds like he fell off the altar and died. Is that right?

KATABUCHI: You would think so. The whole family said the same thing: 'Yoichi must have been playing around and climbed up on the altar, but his foot slipped, and he fell.'

But it just doesn't seem right to me. For one thing, I don't think a child could have climbed up onto that altar on their own.

Katabuchi quickly drew something in the blank space next to the floor plan.

KATABUCHI: That ledge about halfway up was roughly level with my shoulder at the time, so probably quite a bit higher than a metre. Below that, there was nothing you could have used as a foothold. I don't think I could have climbed it, and Yoichi was shorter than me, and not at all athletic, so I just don't believe he could have got up there alone.

AUTHOR: I see.

KATABUCHI: On top of that, Yoichi was scared of the altar. So was I, for that matter, but there was something more to his fear. Something odd. He wouldn't even look in its direction when we walked down the hall. And they think he tried to climb it? Not a chance.

KURIHARA: Did anyone else in your family point this out?

KATABUCHI: No one. Everyone just seemed to accept it as an accident. When I tried to voice my own doubts, I was told off. 'Children should be silent and listen' is what they told me, and no one paid me any more mind.

KURIHARA: And what did the doctor say?

KATABUCHI: I don't remember exactly, but I think it was something like, 'He struck his head and injured his brain.'

AUTHOR: What they call a cerebral contusion, I suppose.

KURIHARA: Did he show any doubt about the cause of death?

KATABUCHI: Not that I noticed. The doctor was a very old man, shuffling about and mumbling. I honestly don't know how reliable his judgement was.

KURIHARA: And what about the police?

KATABUCHI: They weren't involved. Aunt Misaki did suggest, once, that we ought to call them and have them investigate, but everyone else was firmly against the idea, so she gave up. I think she was the only one who felt unconvinced by the story.

AUTHOR: But it's completely normal to call the police when there's a death. Why would anyone object?

KATABUCHI: I don't know. But . . . I have this nagging feeling that they were all hiding something. It's hard to explain.

KURIHARA: So, for some reason they didn't want to involve the police.

There was a long silence. None of us wanted to say it, but the most likely reason was obvious. If the death wasn't an accident, then that left suicide or murder. From Katabuchi's story, there clearly was something strange going on in her family. Could they have been covering for someone? If so, who? And to what end?

## THE PROBLEM OF TIME

KURIHARA: If we can't trust the doctor, and there was no police investigation of the scene, then all we have to go on is your memory, Ms Katabuchi. Can you tell us about the day before Yoichi died?

KATABUCHI: I can. That day, we all went to visit Uncle Kimihiko's grave in the morning. Well, all of us except Grandfather. He stayed at home. On the way back, we went shopping and stopped by the park. We didn't get home until the evening.

After that, we had dinner before taking turns in the bath. Then everyone went to their own rooms.

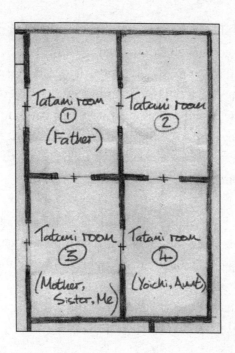

I played a game with my sister and Yoichi in room ③. After a while, Yoichi felt sleepy and went back to his room, ④. Now that I think about it, that was the last time I saw him alive.

KURIHARA: Do you remember roughly what time that was?

KATABUCHI: Let's see . . . the evening news was on NHK, so I think it must have been just before nine o'clock. Ayano and I kept playing for another thirty minutes or so, until Mum told us to go to bed. I grumbled but crawled into my futon. Ayano fell asleep immediately, but I wasn't sleepy at all, for some reason. I ended up staying awake until around four a.m., just lying there.

KURIHARA: Did you notice anything unusual in all that time? Like, someone coming into your room?

116

KATABUCHI: No, nothing happened while I was awake.

KURIHARA: I see . . .

Kurihara sat thinking for a moment, then pointed his pen at the floor plan.

KURIHARA: Ms Katabuchi, you said that the fusuma between ① and ② wouldn't open, right?

KATABUCHI: Yes.

KURIHARA: So then, for Yoichi to get out into the corridor, he would have had to go through your room. But you said no one came into your room while you were awake. In which case, he must have died after you fell asleep, around four. His body was found around five, which means his time of death lay in that hour between four and five.

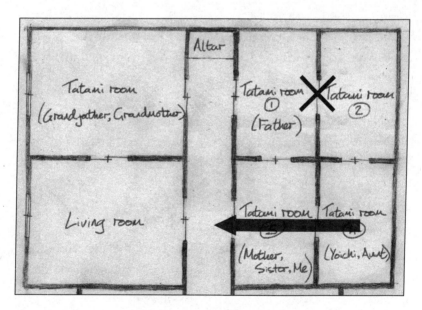

Somehow, Kurihara's scenario didn't seem right to me. I had the feeling it didn't fit with something we'd heard earlier. I thought back a few minutes, then it came to me.

AUTHOR: Pardon me, Ms Katabuchi, but just now, when you talked about Yoichi's body, you said it was 'ice-cold to the touch', didn't you?

KATABUCHI: Yes.

AUTHOR: I have interviewed quite a few doctors in my time, and this topic has come up before. Human bodies cool at a relatively fixed rate after death. If I remember correctly, without massive blood loss, they stay warm for two hours or so. How much blood do you think Yoichi lost?

KATABUCHI: There was some dried blood around the wound on his head, but not all that much. Wait . . . are you saying . . . ?

AUTHOR: Yoichi probably died more than two hours before his body was found.

KATABUCHI: But . . .

KURIHARA: Yoichi should have been in his room at that time. There's an inconsistency.

It seemed Yoichi had somehow reached the altar in the corridor without passing through Yuzuki's room. How? I stared at the floor plan, deep in thought.

KURIHARA: I can think of one possibility.

KATABUCHI: You can?

KURIHARA: If we assume that Yoichi fell from the altar and died, then the timings don't add up. But what if he died somewhere else?

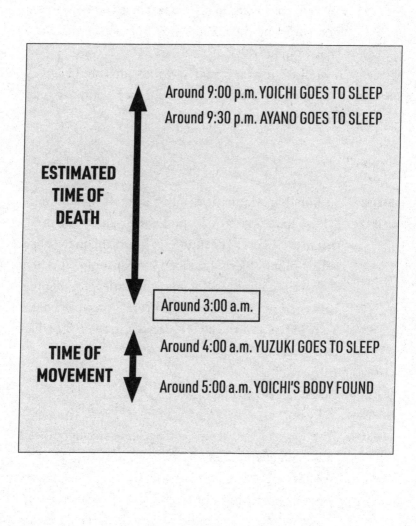

AUTHOR:     Like in his room?

KURIHARA:   Right. Let's say, three hours before his body was dis-
            covered, Yoichi died in his room. Then, sometime after
            four, someone moved his body in front of the altar.
            That would make it all fit.

AUTHOR:     It would, but who would have done that, and why?

KURIHARA:   I say it was the murderer, because they wanted to hide
            the cause of death.

Murderer . . .

AUTHOR:     So, you don't think it was an accident. It was murder.

KURIHARA:   I don't have any proof, but it's really the only thing
            that makes sense. The murderer hit Yoichi on the head
            with a blunt object and killed him in room ④. Then
            they waited until Ms Katabuchi fell asleep, sometime
            between four and five in the morning, then placed the
            body in front of the altar to make the death look like
            an accident.

KATABUCHI:  I see.

KURIHARA:   But, no, that can't be right.

AUTHOR:     Why not?

KURIHARA:   As soon as I said it, I could see that my hypothesis
            was inadequate. There are two serious flaws. The first
            relates to the identity of the murderer. If my theory
            were correct, the murderer must have been in the
            room with Yoichi after he went to bed, which means
            it could only have been Aunt Misaki. I would never
            go so far as to say that a mother is incapable of killing
            her own son, but she was the only one in the family

120

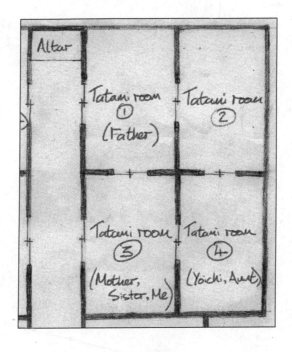

who wanted to call the police. That alone makes her an unlikely culprit.

The other flaw is the problem of sound. If Yoichi had been killed in his room, then surely Ms Katabuchi would have heard something. Did you hear anything?

KATABUCHI: No, nothing. It was quiet up until I fell asleep.

AUTHOR: So, what then?

KURIHARA: So, Yoichi did not die in his room. My hypothesis was half-wrong. But I still think I'm right that the murderer moved his body in front of the altar to hide the cause of death.

In short, I think it happened like this. The murderer removed Yoichi from his room somehow and killed him elsewhere in the house. Then, they put the body in front of the altar. The questions are, how did they get Yoichi out of the room, and where did they kill him?

Just then, Katabuchi sat up straight, as if she'd remembered something.

KATABUCHI: Wait. Now I remember. Grandmother said she heard something in the night.

AUTHOR: Like what?

KATABUCHI: She said she heard a thumping sound from the next room, in the middle of the night, around one. She went to look, but everything seemed normal. And no one was in front of the altar then. We didn't pay it any mind since it didn't seem to have anything to do with Yoichi.

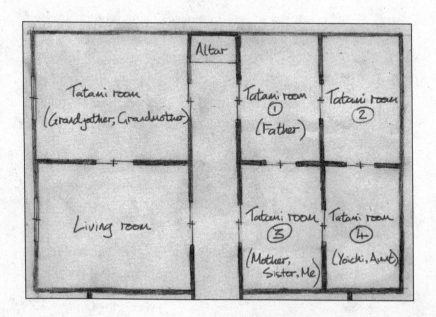

KURIHARA: The next room . . . you mean, the living room?
KATABUCHI: I suppose so.

Something was wrong with her grandmother's story, but I couldn't put my finger on it. Then, staring at the floor plan, something jumped out at me.

AUTHOR: Why did she go out into the corridor to check the living room?

KATABUCHI: What do you mean?

AUTHOR: Your grandmother checked the next room to investigate the noise but she said that no one was in front of the altar. If she could see the altar, she must have gone out into the corridor. But there's a door between her room and the living room.

If she could have gone straight into the living room, it seems strange to me that she stepped out into the corridor.

KATABUCHI: You're right, that is strange. Well then, maybe by 'the next room' she meant the tatami room over the corridor.

AUTHOR: That would be room ①, where your father was sleeping. In which case, I imagine your father would have mentioned hearing something, or her coming in to check.

KATABUCHI: You're right.

AUTHOR: What do you think, Kurihara?

Kurihara sat silent for a while, glaring at the floor plan. Eventually, he began to speak in a quiet voice.

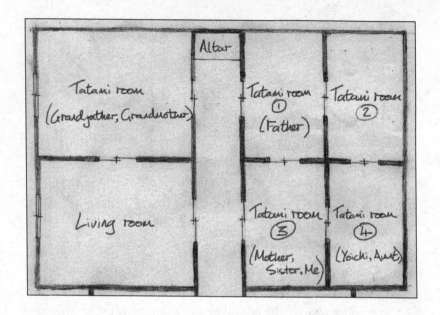

KURIHARA: That was well spotted. You're absolutely right. The 'next room' can't have meant the living room or the tatami mat room across the corridor.

KATABUCHI: Then, what other room could it be?

KURIHARA: I think it must be a room missing from this floor plan.

KATABUCHI: What?

## THE HIDDEN ROOM

AUTHOR: Meaning what, exactly?

KURIHARA: This is just the layout of the house as Ms Katabuchi remembers it. Which means things she didn't see, such as hidden rooms, would not be included.

AUTHOR: You think the house had hidden rooms?

KURIHARA: Based on all we've heard so far, that seems the only possible conclusion.

124

Kurihara picked up a pencil and added a single line to the floor plan.

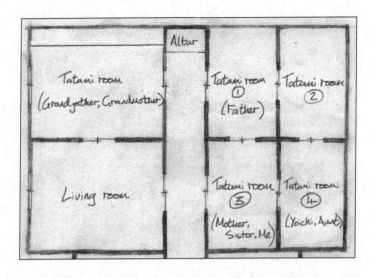

AUTHOR:      What is that?

KURIHARA:    I think there may have been another room next to your
             grandmother's room, hidden behind a wall.

AUTHOR:      That would explain her 'next room' comment, but why
             do you think it was located there?

KURIHARA:    That's simple. With a square room like this, a 'next
             room' can only be in one of four places.

             To the north, east, west or south.

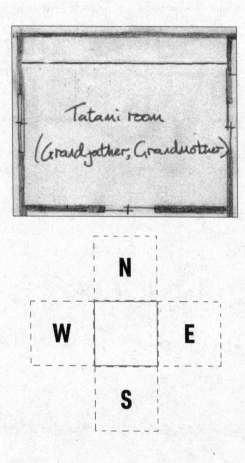

In the case of the grandparents' room, all the walls but one have a door or window in them. If there were a hidden room, it would have to be on the side with no doors or windows.

AUTHOR: But why have a hidden room at all?

KATABUCHI: For confinement.

AUTHOR: Confinement?!

KATABUCHI: If this house was built for the same purpose as the ones in Tokyo and Saitama, then it would have a confinement room somewhere too.

KURIHARA: I agree. And that room would have a child like X in it.


X . . . the child raised to murder. Which meant, this house was also . . . At the realization, my thoughts inevitably linked Yoichi and Hiroto.


AUTHOR: You aren't saying the child killed Yoichi?

KURIHARA: I think that's unlikely. The child prisoner escaped, killed Yoichi and placed his body in front of the altar . . . then went right back into its prison? Either that, or your grandparents let the child out deliberately so that it could carry out the murder, and I can't imagine that they wanted Yoichi dead. I'd say that someone, for some reason, took Yoichi to the confinement room and killed him there.

AUTHOR: But how would anyone get in and out of that room?

KURIHARA: Your grandmother went out into the corridor to check this 'next room'. So, the entrance must have been somewhere in the corridor. And there's only one place

127

in the corridor that could connect to the hidden room. The altar.

KATABUCHI: What?!

KURIHARA: When you described it, you said, 'It took up the full width of the corridor. Not a gap between it and the walls.'

I think, in truth, it must have been something like this.

Kurihara drew some more on the floor plan.

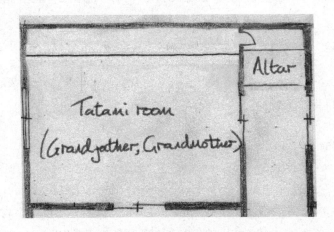

AUTHOR: You think there was a space behind it?

KURIHARA: They hid the door leading to the hidden room behind the altar. It was taller than you were, right, Ms Katabuchi? You were still a child, so it was too high for you to see anything behind it.

KATABUCHI: But then, how would anyone have got to the entrance? I can't imagine my grandmother clambering over the altar.

128

KURIHARA: You said yourself that there was a big painting of a mandala inside the altar. I suspect a door was hidden behind it. So, you would open up the altar to get through the hidden door and into the confinement room. And someone who knew about this took Yoichi there and killed him.

AUTHOR: But, why there?

KURIHARA: The answer to that question will be the key to unlocking this murder and the mystery of these houses.


## THE TRUE SHAPE

KURIHARA: Let's go over the order of events.

At around one in the morning, the murderer took the sleeping Yoichi out of his room. The problem is, how did they get to room ④ without passing through room ③? They used the tricks of the house.

Those tricks, of course, were all tied to it being a murder house. The houses in Tokyo and Saitama had hidden routes connecting the confinement room with the murder room. This house must have had the same. So then, where is the murder room in this house?

Ms Katabuchi, room ② was never used, is that right?

KATABUCHI: Yes.

KURIHARA: My mind keeps returning to it. Yoichi and his mother were in room ④. Yoichi was growing up and you'd think room ② would have made a perfect study or playroom. But, for some reason, it was kept empty. I think that must have been because it was built for a

129

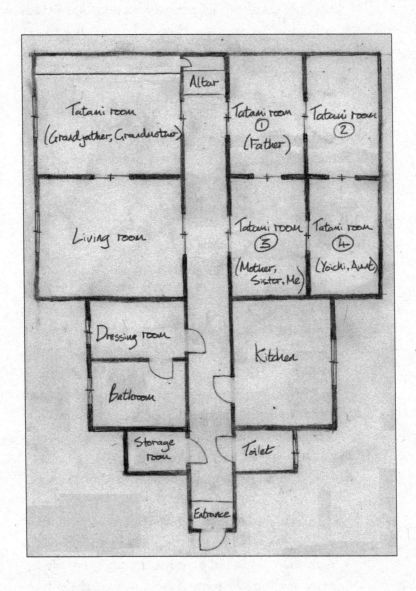

specific purpose. I believe this room served the same purpose as the bathrooms in the Saitama and Tokyo houses. In other words, it was a murder room.

And if that's the case, there has to be a hidden route connecting it to the confinement room. Of course, it wouldn't be drawn on the floor plan. However, I think it's easy to imagine.

Kurihara drew some more.

KURIHARA: Right. So, behind the altar are spaces on each side. The one to the left is the confinement room, and on the right is the passage leading to the murder room. The murderer used that passage to get to Yoichi's room via room ②.

KATABUCHI: But how was the passage connected to room ②? There wasn't anything in there that could have hidden a door.

KURIHARA: I can think of one possibility.

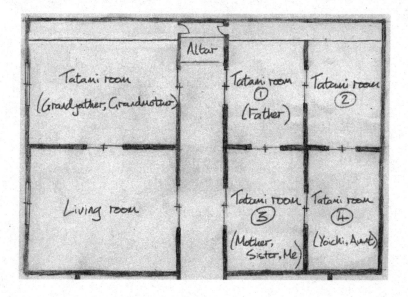

Kurihara pointed at the jammed fusuma.

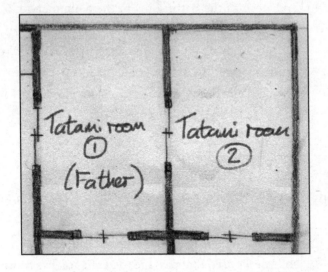

KURIHARA: I wonder if these fusuma really were permanently jammed.

Couldn't they just have been locked from the inside?

KATABUCHI: Inside where?

KURIHARA: Ms Katabuchi, I'm so sorry to be drawing all over this floor plan that you worked so hard on. But I think this is the last thing I'll change.

At that, Kurihara redrew the jammed fusuma.

KURIHARA: I think this was the true layout of the house. There were actually two fusuma, with a small space in between.

They were both locked from the inside, so that from the outside they appeared to be a single, jammed fusuma. And that's the trick that had you fooled, Ms Katabuchi.

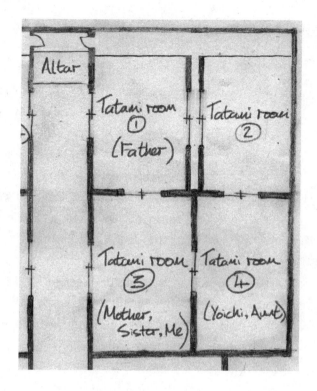

KATABUCHI: I can't . . . what?

KURIHARA: Let's imagine how the house was used. The owners would invite their targets over to stay and put them in room ②. They would wait for the right moment, then send the child through the passage from the confinement room. The child would creep into the space between the fusuma, slide open the doors leading into room ②, then sneak in and kill the guest.

It's the same basic principle from before. Those two other houses were just slightly different versions of this setup.

KATABUCHI: It can't be . . .

KURIHARA: And the murderer thought they could use that trick to kill Yoichi.

The murderer went through the altar from the corridor into the secret passageway, then snuck into room ④, where Aunt Misaki and Yoichi were deeply asleep, via room ②. They took Yoichi and carried him back through the passage, all the way to the confinement room. Lots of young kids don't wake if you pick them up carefully when they're sleeping. Once they were in the confinement room, they killed him.

AUTHOR: Why kill him there, though?

KURIHARA: There are two reasons.

The first was that the murderer feared Yoichi might wake up. If he did, he might have called out or started struggling and woken the rest of the household, which would have ruined the whole plan. On the other hand, there wasn't time to carry him far away, and it would have been impractical to take the sleeping child through the narrow altar opening in any case.

The second reason was to muffle the sound of Yoichi being beaten to death.

This hidden passage connects several rooms, so no matter where the murder happened, someone would be sure to hear something. The thing they most wanted to avoid was waking up Aunt Misaki because she'd immediately notice Yoichi was gone.

That's why the murderer chose the confinement room. It was the furthest they could get from where Misaki was sleeping. Of course, if the child prisoner

134

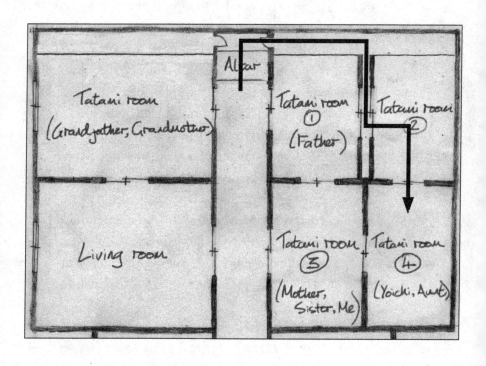

witnessed the crime, it might lead to problems later, so maybe they did it just outside the room's door.

At any rate, the noise woke your grandmother, who immediately assumed it had been made by the child prisoner and went through the altar door to check. I suspect the murderer had foreseen that possibility and carried Yoichi's body back through the passage to room ② to avoid being seen. When your grandmother saw nothing amiss, she returned to her room, and the murderer followed her through the altar to the hallway. There, they left Yoichi's body in front of the altar, before returning to their own room. After that, they just had to wait until someone found the body.

AUTHOR: I can see how it all fits together, but . . . isn't it all a little far-fetched? It's so convoluted. I get the feeling that if the police had investigated, they'd have seen through the whole thing immediately. There are just too many moving parts and opportunities for something to go wrong, or for evidence to be left behind.

KURIHARA: You're right. And the murderer put Yoichi's body in front of the altar precisely so that the police wouldn't investigate.

AUTHOR: What's that supposed to mean?

KURIHARA: Think about it. If the police had come to the house, they would naturally have investigated the supposed scene of death—the altar. Inevitably, they would have discovered the secret passage, the confinement room and the child. All the Katabuchi family's dark secrets would have been brought to light. They would have wanted to avoid that at all costs.

136

So, the murderer had counted on the family coming up with the accident story to cover up the murder.

KATABUCHI: That's it. That's why, when Aunt Misaki tried to get someone to call them, everyone was so desperate to stop her.

KURIHARA: Maybe they all knew his death wasn't an accident, but they reached an unspoken agreement to put up a front to protect the family secret. As Yoichi's mother, though, your aunt was simply too upset to consider such things, but I doubt the murderer was worried about that. They were essentially blackmailing the Katabuchis, and they knew the rest of the family would prevent her from contacting the authorities.

AUTHOR: Who could the murderer have been, then?

KURIHARA: Let's try a process of elimination.

First, Ms Katabuchi's mother is in the clear, because she was sleeping in the room with her and her sister. Her grandfather could hardly walk, so he's out, as is her grandmother, who was sleeping in the same room as him. It's just possible they were in on it together, but if so, I can't see why she would have told that story about hearing something in the middle of the night. Which leaves . . .

KATABUCHI: My father . . . he's the only one.

Katabuchi said it herself. Her father must have been the murderer. It was not the kind of truth that most people could have accepted so calmly, but she seemed surprisingly untroubled as she uttered the words.

KATABUCHI: The truth is, my father began to fall apart after the accident. Or, the murder. He shut himself away in his room and took to drinking all day. I think, somewhere in the back of my mind, I might have suspected he was somehow involved in Yoichi's death all along.

AUTHOR: But what possible motive could he have had?

KATABUCHI: I don't remember ever seeing them so much as talk to one another. I mean, I didn't get the feeling my father disliked Yoichi or anything, but . . . I don't know. I can't even begin to imagine a motive.

KURIHARA: Could it have something to do with the line of inheritance?

KATABUCHI: What inheritance?

KURIHARA: They might have fallen on hard times, but the Katabuchis were once a grand family. Perhaps carrying on the family name still held some value. There were three grandchildren: Yoichi, Ayano and you. One of you would take over as head of the Katabuchi family and inherit the estate and all its benefits.

As a boy, Yoichi would have had the strongest claim. But if he were to die, then the succession would go to your sister or you. As the eldest, of course, your sister Ayano would have come first. For some reason, your father must have wanted your sister to become the head of the Katabuchi family.

Come to think of it, when Ayano got married, her husband chose to take the Katabuchi name, rather than her taking his name. Which meant he was adopted into the family. But—

138

AUTHOR: Hang on, though. Would he really have killed his own nephew over the family name?

KURIHARA: It sounds wild, but we already know the Katabuchi family is not a normal one. I would not be surprised if there were some other, deeply weird explanation we can't even imagine.

AUTHOR: I see . . .

KURIHARA: And from there, it's not hard to imagine why your sister suddenly vanished in your childhood, Ms Katabuchi. She was being brainwashed at your grandparents' house.

AUTHOR: Brainwashed?!

KURIHARA: The Katabuchi family has been murdering people for generations. I don't know why, but it has become a tradition. Your sister had to take up that burden.

But if you take someone raised in a normal home and tell them, 'From now on, you're going to use a child to kill,' they wouldn't be able to do it. And so, the successor to the Katabuchi name has to be kept close to the family head from a young age and brainwashed into going along with their murderous ritual. Of course, this is all speculation.

Just then, there was a knock at the door of the meeting room, and a voice said, 'Pardon me, time is almost up.' I glanced down at my watch and saw it was already well after six. We concluded our discussion and got ready to leave.

·   ·   ·

Outside, the streetlights were coming on one by one. The three of us walked towards the station.

AUTHOR: I was wondering, Ms Katabuchi, are your grandparents still alive and well?

KATABUCHI: I honestly couldn't tell you. I haven't been back to their house since Yoichi's death. I basically cut all ties with my family after I moved out. Apart from that short-lived exchange with Ayano, I'm not in touch with anyone.

AUTHOR: I see . . .

KATABUCHI: But after what we discussed today, I've decided to go back there.

AUTHOR: Do you know the address?

KATABUCHI: No. But I'm sure my mother does. I have to go and see her one more time. And this time . . . I'm going to learn the truth about my sister. Wherever she is, she must be miserable. I want to help her.

After a short walk, we reached the station. There were few people around, it being a Sunday evening.

We said our goodbyes at the ticket gates and went our separate ways.


## AN UNEXPECTED CALL

I arrived home just after eight. I was exhausted. I had no appetite, so I decided to take a bath and get to bed. Just then, my phone rang. It was Katabuchi.

AUTHOR:     Hello. Has something happened?

KATABUCHI: Actually, I was wondering . . .

She sounded nervous.

KATABUCHI: Just now, after we said goodbye, I received a call from
           my mother. She said there was something she wants to
           tell me about my sister. That she wants to meet soon.
           As soon as possible. So, I'm going to see her tomorrow
           evening.

AUTHOR:     That's unexpected. And quick!

KATABUCHI: It is. Anyway. I'm sorry for asking you this out of the
           blue, but . . . would you come with me?

AUTHOR:     What? Me?

KATABUCHI: Yes. Of course, I know you must be busy, so I'll under-
           stand if you can't.

I looked at my calendar and saw that I had nothing planned for
the next evening.

AUTHOR:     I'd be happy to come, of course. But are you certain
            you want me to tag along? I'm sure she would prefer
            to speak to you alone.

KATABUCHI: Don't worry about that. I've already mentioned it
           to her. And, personally, I'd very much like you to be
           there. For a long time our relationship was so bad she
           wouldn't even let me in her home. Now, she wants me
           to come over to talk about Ayano? There's something
           strange going on. I'm a little embarrassed to say it, but
           I'm afraid to go alone.

AUTHOR:   I can understand that. Would you like me to check if
          Kurihara can come?
KATABUCHI: If it's no bother.

We agreed a time to meet and hung up.

I got in touch with Kurihara. 'I'd like to come too,' he said, 'but work won't let me.' Of course, the next day was a Monday, and Kurihara had a nine-to-five job, unlike me. I wasn't happy about it, but it couldn't be helped.

He made me promise to keep him posted, and that was that.

# CHAPTER FOUR

# House of Chains

## THE LETTER

The next evening at five, I met Katabuchi at Omiya Station.

KATABUCHI: I really am sorry to keep putting you out like this.
AUTHOR:    It's fine. No need to apologize. I want to find out what
           happened to your sister, too. So, where does your
           mother live, exactly?
KATABUCHI: In Kumagaya. We can take the Takasaki Line straight
           there.

On the train, Katabuchi told me more about her mother.

Yoshie Katabuchi (née Matsuoka) was born in Shimane Prefecture in the far west of Japan and moved to Saitama Prefecture when she married her first husband, Yuzuki's late father. By now she had already divorced her second husband and lived alone in a flat she owned in Kumagaya City, Saitama Prefecture.

We arrived at the station after a thirty-minute journey.

A short walk brought us within sight of Yoshie's flat. Katabuchi stopped and took a few deep breaths, as if to steady her nerves, and we went in.

We took the elevator to the fifth floor and walked down a corridor to the room second from the end. The nameplate read 'Katabuchi'. Yuzuki took another deep breath and rang the doorbell.

Soon, the door swung open to reveal a petite woman who looked to be in her mid-fifties. Yoshie Katabuchi. Upon seeing me, she bowed deeply and said, 'Do pardon us for bringing you all this way.' She glanced at Yuzuki, briefly meeting her gaze before both women quickly averted their eyes in discomfort.

She led us to the living groom. A framed photograph propped on the TV stand caught my eye. It was grainy and low resolution, like something taken on an old digital camera, and showed the family together. It looked like they were at an amusement park somewhere. Yoshie was there, looking much younger, and a man who must have been Yuzuki's father. Between them, two young girls stood making peace signs at the camera. They must have been Yuzuki and her sister, Ayano.

We sat around the living room coffee table. Yoshie served tea, but Yuzuki did not touch hers. She simply sat in silence with her face lowered. The uncomfortable silence dragged on. I felt like I should try to break the ice, but before I could, Yoshie started to speak.

YOSHIE:    I've been worrying about all of this since the last time you came, Yuzuki. I was trying to decide if I should just tell you everything. But I couldn't make up my mind.

She glanced at the photograph on the TV stand.

YOSHIE:    Long ago, I promised your father and sister never to tell you the truth.

Yuzuki tried to speak, but, overwhelmed, she seemed to choke on her words. She took a sip of tea, gathering herself, and finally found her voice. When she spoke, she was distant.

YUZUKI: Is this . . . about that house?

YOSHIE: So, you've figured that much out. Yes, it is. I never wanted you to know any of this. I wanted you, at least, to escape our family curse. But . . . well, things have changed.

Yoshie laid an envelope on the table.

It was addressed to her, and the return address began with 'Keita Katabuchi.'

YUZUKI: Keita? Ayano's husband?

YOSHIE: That's right. It arrived yesterday.

Yuzuki picked up the envelope. The letter inside was several pages long, handwritten in careful characters. It read:

To Mrs Yoshie Katabuchi,

I apologize for writing to you like this. My name is Keita Katabuchi.

Seven years ago, I married your daughter, Ayano. I regret that we never had the chance to tell you ourselves before now. The timing never seemed appropriate.

I am writing you now with an urgent plea for help. Ayano and I are in desperate need. We understand the difficulty of what we are asking, but we hope you will find it in your heart to help us.

I believe that, so you can better understand our current situation, I should let you know everything we have been through so far. The story will be long, but I beg for your patience.

147

Ayano and I met in 2009.

I was a high school student in —— Prefecture. I did not enjoy my time at school, where I was the target of class bullies.

At first, they simply made a point of ignoring me, or hiding my things, but the bullying grew worse by the day. One morning, I arrived at school to find my desk drenched with water. As I stood there, miserable, trying to mop it dry with everyone else staring and leering at me, only one other person picked up a towel and tried to help. Ayano.

She was a quiet girl, and never went out of her way to connect with people, but I could see that she was kind and decent, and had a brave heart.

After that, Ayano came to my aid time and again, and I did all I could to return the favour. I was a good student, so I tutored her in her weaker subjects before tests.

We became a couple in the spring of our second year. I told Ayano how I felt about her and asked her to be my girlfriend. When she said yes, I was so happy that it felt like I was walking on air for days.

The school he mentioned was in the same prefecture as Grandfather Katabuchi's house. It seemed Kurihara could have been right about Ayano being taken there to be brainwashed.

But it also seemed she had been allowed at least some freedom, if she had gone to school, started a relationship with this bullied young man and eventually got married.

So far, the story was unexpectedly heartwarming. But the letter was not finished and soon took a darker turn.

However, not long after we started dating, I began to notice some puzzling behaviour in Ayano. Every day, as soon as school finished, she would immediately hurry out to the car waiting to take her home, and I wouldn't hear a single word from her until the next morning. Even stranger was that she would never tell me anything about her family, her home or where she grew up. I know it sounds overblown, but I got the feeling that she was hiding some dark secret.

I finally learnt what it was in the winter before our graduation.

We sat in a corner of an empty classroom and, after making me swear I would never breathe a word to another soul, Ayano told me about the Offering of the Left Hand.

YUZUKI:   What? The offering of . . . the left hand?
YOSHIE:   That is what has led our family to ruin.

Yoshie stood up and went to the next room, then returned holding a small lockbox. She opened the lid, and a foul, musty odour filled the air. The box contained a tattered bundle of discoloured paper. It looked ancient. It was covered in hand-brushed characters in an old-fashioned style I could not read.

YOSHIE:   It was over thirty years ago that I learnt that same secret. I had come to meet your father's parents just before we got married.

Your grandfather, my father-in-law, showed this box to me and told me about the Offering of the Left Hand. It is a deeply unpleasant story, and I found it so odd that he would share such a thing with his son's fiancée, but I was young and took it for some kind of tasteless joke. But eventually, I understood just how serious he was. This is a tradition that has been passed down for decades and binds the Katabuchi family like chains.

Here, I offer a summary of those portions of Yoshie's story fit for publication.

## BROTHERS

The Katabuchi family once lived in —— Prefecture, where it made its fortune running a variety of businesses. The greatest single contributor to its success was named Kaei Katabuchi, who headed the family from 1899 to 1915.

Kaei was a bold man, gifted with outstanding business acumen, and he managed to expand the family business to a huge scale. However, soon after his fiftieth birthday, he fell chronically ill and decided to step away from the front lines of the business. He would have to name a successor.

Kaei had three children: Soichiro, Chizuru and Seikichi.

Soichiro, the oldest son, was an introverted child, nothing like his father. He was an odd boy altogether, and a little slow. He got on well with his younger sister, Chizuru, though. Even as he grew older, they would play house and other games of make-believe together.

The youngest son, Seikichi, was his complete opposite. He was an outgoing, energetic child who excelled both in study and in sports. Even from a young age he exhibited courage and

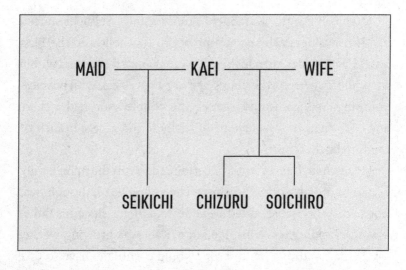

```
MAID ———— KAEI ———— WIFE
        |            |
        |      ┌─────┴─────┐
        |      |           |
     SEIKICHI  CHIZURU  SOICHIRO
```

leadership, and everyone knew that his was the right hand to take the tiller of the Katabuchi business.

And yet, Kaei, to the surprise of all, chose his oldest son, Soichiro, to succeed him. The reason lay in Seikichi's birth.

The truth was, Kaei's two older children were born to his wife, while Seikichi alone was his son by a maid who had worked in the house. He was, in other words, an illegitimate child. Kaei shied away from allowing such a son to take control of the family purely out of concern for appearances. Even so, he knew as well as anyone that Soichiro had no aptitude for business. It seems his plan was to install Soichiro as a figurehead while allowing Seikichi to have the true run of things.

However, such a plan was not to be.

Seikichi refused to stay in Soichiro's shadow. He left home and struck out on his own. His feelings are understandable. It was as if his own father had said, 'You are unfit to stand at the head of this family because of your birth.' He must have been furious.

After leaving the Katabuchi family estate, Seikichi started his own business. The economic boom that followed the First World War helped turn his venture into a massive success within a few short years. At the young age of twenty-two, with business booming, Seikichi found a wife. The couple soon had a child, and with that, he was able to officially found a new branch of the Katabuchi family.

Meanwhile, Kaei essentially continued to run the main family, as a kind of 'advisor' to Soichiro. The young head, though, was not necessarily satisfied with the arrangement, since his father was still holding the reins. He knew Kaei was growing weaker by the day, and that he, the son, would eventually have to take charge in truth. So, he dedicated himself to studying and learning the family business. Kaei was proud to see it.

However, there was one more thing that worried Kaei. That was the problem of Soichiro's marriage.

Soichiro had been a late bloomer, and even at the age of twenty-four he still had never been close to a woman. It was a clear problem for the future succession of the Katabuchi family. Finally, Kaei decided he would pick a bride for his son himself.

His choice was Ushio Takama, a woman who worked on the family estate. Ushio had come to serve the family at the age of twelve and had shown great aptitude for household work such as cleaning or cooking. Kaei was charmed by her sincerity and work ethic. When she turned sixteen, he made her Soichiro's personal attendant.

Three years later, Kaei judged her ideal to become Soichiro's wife. They were of a similar age and, from her work, she was already deeply familiar with the young man's character.

# USHIO

Ushio Takama was then nineteen years old. She had been born into a poor family, and her parents had died when she was still a child. She had then been passed from one relative to another, living in poverty so terrible that she had sometimes eaten roadside weeds to quiet her hunger pangs. When she started working at the Katabuchi house, she found herself once again at the very bottom of the ranks and was abused morning to night by her superiors.

And then came the day that changed everything.

She married Soichiro, the head of the household. It was a new life entirely. She went from a lowly maid to mistress of the house. Everything she could ever want was hers for the asking. Ushio was ecstatic.

A few days after the couple were married, Kaei passed away quietly, as if in relief at finally setting the future of his house in order.

In public, Soichiro's new wife Ushio lived out her dreams, delighting in gourmet food and exquisite clothing. Where once she had been forced to bow to all, where once she had suffered and hungered, now her days were filled with pleasure.

Even amid the joys of her new luxury, though, one thing bothered her in private. It was her husband's attitude towards her. Soichiro was kind to Ushio, but he did not treat her as a wife. They had not been together as a man and woman once, even after their marriage.

One night, Ushio woke to find that her husband was not in bed beside her.

He did not return for almost an hour.

She soon discovered that this was a nightly occurrence. Growing suspicious, Ushio eventually resolved to follow Soichiro.

When she did, she learnt that his nightly destination was the room of his sister, Chizuru.

## PERIL

Around the same time, clouds began to gather over the main family's business affairs.

The main family's success had been entirely sustained by Kaei's singular leadership. Try as he might, Soichiro could never measure up to his late father. Many of the outstanding employees Kaei brought on could see no future for the family and left, one after another. Business began to suffer. Then, a few years later, came the final blow.

Chizuru became pregnant with Soichiro's child.

The family fell into chaos. If the world learnt of the incest between the head of the family and his own sister, the Katabuchi name would be irrevocably stained. Everyone in the family's inner circle frantically tried to hide the truth.

But one person did learn of it. Soichiro's half-brother, Seikichi.

Seikichi's reaction was unexpected. He forced his way into the house and rebuked Soichiro in front of the whole staff.

'How could I let the Katabuchi name sit in the hands of an imbecile who would commit such indecency with his own sister? You were never fit to be head of this family,' he ranted.

The mere head of the branch family marching in and shouting at the master of the main family? Such brazen behaviour was utterly unacceptable by the values of the day. And yet, there were those deeply involved in the family businesses who had long been dissatisfied with Soichiro's performance. Many silently agreed with Seikichi.

Seikichi seized on the weakness of his half-brother's leadership. Through hard-headed negotiation and gentle coaxing, he managed to buy off key figures in the main family. Soichiro lacked the ability to stop him. Soon, through means fair or foul, Seikichi managed to wrest control of the majority of the family's stakes and holdings.

All that he left for the main family was the manor and surrounding estate, a small remnant of the fortune and a few employees. And so, Seikichi had taken his revenge on the family and brother who he felt had humiliated him.

The one who suffered most from the loss was Soichiro's wife. The idle days of luxury Ushio had spent were now over, and she saw herself headed back towards wretched poverty. And as Soichiro's wife, she could never go over to the branch family.

A lonely mountain estate falling into ruin, a loveless marriage and a life alone with Soichiro and his sister, pregnant with his child. It was hell, and Ushio's mental state crumbled.

The first to notice her growing disturbance was a housemaid. When she would call out to Ushio, the woman's responses grew weak and sporadic, only to give way to the selfish tantrums of a greedy child. This petulance stood in stark contrast to Ushio's former quiet stoicism.

Eventually, she would sit vacantly all day long, her stupor broken only by violent, irrational outbursts of weeping and self-harm as she raked her own body with her long fingernails.

Soichiro must have felt some guilt, for he soon took to seeing to Ushio's daily needs himself. This kindness, though, precipitated a tragedy.

155

One day, Ushio declared that she wished to eat persimmon.

Soichiro brought one to her room. He peeled and sliced it, but Ushio stopped eating after only a few slices. Soichiro left the rest by her bedside. He failed to notice that he had also left the knife.

A few minutes later, Soichiro felt a vague uneasiness. He hurried back to Ushio's room, but it was too late.

The sight that greeted him was shocking. Ushio was lying in the middle of the room, drenched in blood, surrounded by countless bloody handprints covering the tatami mats.

Ushio had thrust the knife through her left wrist and then slammed that hand, spouting blood, onto the mats over and over. She did it until the bone gave way and the flesh ripped, leaving her left hand dangling by only a thin flap of skin.

It was unclear whether she had meant to kill herself, or whether it was simply an escalation of her self-harm. Soichiro, though, was convinced that her death was his fault. His grief was profound.

## TWINS

A few months after Ushio died, Chizuru gave birth to twin boys.

Soichiro was stunned. The first child was born healthy, with all fingers and toes intact. The second son, though, was missing his left hand. It was a dreadful coincidence.

Nowadays, we know that incest between close family members can lead to the expression of recessive genes and birth defects in children. And, in fact, there had been several people born with such a disability in the Katabuchi family before.

But Soichiro, of course, knew none of this, and he could not help but be reminded of the late Ushio and her severed left hand. He grew increasingly convinced she had laid a dying curse on them all.

Soichiro and Chizuru took their children from shrine to shrine and temple to temple, seeking to have the curse lifted.

The abbot of a Buddhist temple told them that hemp—known as *asa*—and peach—or *momo*—were considered protection against evil in their Buddhist tradition. On his advice, they named the boys Asata and Momota.


## RANKYO

Around the time Asata and Momota turned three, a woman appeared at the old manor. She said her name was Rankyo and claimed to be a mystic shaman.

When Rankyo entered the manor, she told Soichiro, 'This house is filled with a woman's rage. Your wife died here, didn't she?'

Soichiro had not yet told her anything about Ushio, so he was amazed at the woman's mystical insight. Convinced of Rankyo's powers, he didn't hesitate to relate all that had befallen him.

Rankyo listened carefully, then informed him, 'Ushio's hatred is not aimed at you two. All her resentment falls on your brother Seikichi, who took everything from you. Her rage is what has caused Momota's disfigurement and ongoing suffering. If you never get your revenge on Seikichi, then this curse will drag the boy to his death.'

Rankyo taught Soichiro a way to lift Ushio's curse. In short, she told him:

- Momota must be confined in a room where sunlight will not reach him.
- Asata must serve as a warden for Momota, to aid and advise him.
- Soichiro must build a second house away from the main manor and place a shrine to Ushio there.
- During the month of Momota's tenth birthday, Momota must kill one of Seikichi's children.
- The child's left hand must be severed and offered at Ushio's altar, in memorial of her.
- This ritual must be repeated three more times, every following year until Momota's thirteenth birthday.

Rankyo called this ritual the Offering of the Left Hand. Soichiro, terrified of Ushio's wrath, immediately began making preparations for the ritual.

I interrupted Yoshie at that point. I was sorry for stopping her so abruptly, but there was so much I struggled to accept.

AUTHOR:   Pardon me. Who exactly could this Rankyo be? She told Soichiro to build a second house and kill Seikichi's son! Who would trust anyone enough to follow such advice? And why would she have told him those things in the first place?

YOSHIE:   Exactly. I thought the same thing, and that something else must be going on. So, I used my own ways to look into this Rankyo's story. I learnt something fascinating. Rankyo was actually connected to Seikichi.

AUTHOR:   What?!

## THE KATABUCHI BRANCH FAMILY

YOSHIE: It seems Seikichi was quite the ladies' man, and in his twenties he already had five wives, though polygamy had been banned for decades. Rankyo was the sister of his second wife, Shizuko. Rankyo, of course, was a pseudonym. Her real name was Miyako.

AUTHOR: So, you mean . . . Rankyo was actually Seikichi's sister-in-law. What motive could she have for wanting her brother-in-law's son murdered?

YOSHIE: I'm guessing it was once again a matter of succession. At the time, Seikichi had six children. As I understand it, three of them died quite young: the eldest son by his first wife, and the third and fourth sons by his third wife. In the end, the only valid successor left was his second son, by his second wife, Shizuko.

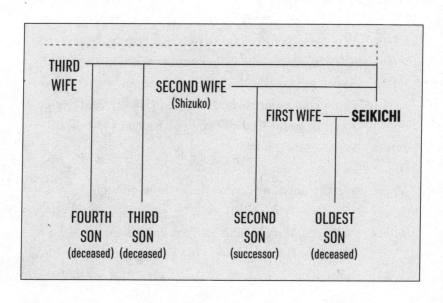

159

AUTHOR:  Are you telling me . . . she wanted her own child to
         inherit, so she . . .

Seikichi had five wives. It was not hard to imagine how they
would fall into constant competition, driven by the fierce urge
to protect their child's interests.

The child of every other wife would be a rival. Shizuko's own
love for her child was twisted into an urge to murder those rivals.
But she couldn't dirty her own hands.

And then she thought of the disgraced main family. She ordered
her sister, Miyako, to play the part of a mystic and earn the trust
of the family head. Soichiro had already been nearly driven to
madness because of his fear of Ushio's curse, so she was able to
persuade him into killing the boys similar in age to her son, and
standing in the way of his succession: the first, third and fourth
sons. And so, they were indeed killed, in that house in the corner
of the estate grounds.

AUTHOR:  Was there still contact between the main family and
         Seikichi, despite the falling out between the two men?
YOSHIE:  Apparently so. I get the feeling that the only way the main
         family could afford to build the second house was through
         funds from the branch family, provided by Shizuko.
AUTHOR:  I see.

There was still something I didn't understand, though.

AUTHOR:  Why did Shizuko and Rankyo charge the children—
         Momota and Asata—with the killing, and not Soichiro
         himself?

YOSHIE: I can't be sure, but I suspect it was a bit of insurance on the part of Shizuko.

AUTHOR: How so?

YOSHIE: If Soichiro himself had committed the murders, he might well have ended up feeling guilty and confessing. Any investigation would have revealed Shizuko's plan. But if the children were the real killers, then Soichiro would have kept his lips sealed to protect them. At least, that's what I think.

AUTHOR: In other words, she did it to keep Soichiro's mouth shut.

YOSHIE: Like I said, though, this is just a supposition.

AUTHOR: And how were relations between the two branches after Rankyo appeared?

YOSHIE: I don't know. Maybe the branch family realized what the main family was doing and broke off all contact. But soon after this time we're talking about, the war broke out. The branch family's businesses were wiped out in the bombings, and they never managed to recover after the war. Seikichi's children were scattered across Japan. The main family, though, hidden away in the mountains like that, was protected from the war and the second house survived unscathed. I'm almost tempted to say, unluckily so.

AUTHOR: Because they passed the Offering of the Left Hand down to later generations?

YOSHIE: Exactly. Soichiro never learnt that it was all just part of Shizuko's dark plan, so he stayed faithful to Rankyo's instructions.

Yoshie took the old bundle of papers from the box and began reading:

### THE OFFERING OF THE LEFT HAND

One. If ever a child lacking a left hand is born to the Katabuchi family, that child shall be kept and nurtured away from the light of the sun.

Two. In the month that the child lacking a left hand reaches its tenth year, it shall take the life of one bearing the blood of Seikichi Katabuchi and remove the left hand of the deceased.

Three. The left hand shall be placed in offering on Ushio's altar, in memorial to her.

Four. The sibling of the child lacking a left hand, or, if there be none such, a relative of similar age, shall be placed as aid.

Five. This ritual shall be repeated thrice more, once a year during the month of the child's birth until the child lacking a left hand has reached the month of its thirteenth birthday.

In modern terms, that means:

If a child with no left hand is born to the Katabuchis, the child is confined in a dark room, to be raised there.

In the month of their tenth birthday, the child must kill a descendant of Seikichi Katabuchi and cut off their left hand.

The severed hand should be offered on Ushio's altar.

The brother or sister of the child is supposed to serve as their warden and helper, or, if they don't have any brother or sister, someone of a similar age in the family must do it.

This ritual must be repeated once a year during the month of the child's birthday until the child's thirteenth year.

YOSHIE: Soichiro wrote out what Rankyo taught him and enshrined her instructions as five family precepts. All the children of his family were forced to learn and abide by them.

AUTHOR: Meaning Asata and Momota.

YOSHIE: To begin with. Soichiro and Chizuru actually had one more child. His name was Shigeharu.

YUZUKI: What did you say?!

The younger Katabuchi, who had sat listening in silence the whole time, could not hold back her shock.

YUZUKI: Shigeharu?! You can't mean . . .

YOSHIE: That's right, Yuzuki. Your grandfather.

## SHIGEHARU

The grandfather that Yuzuki Katabuchi knew when growing up had been taught the Offering of the Left Hand by Soichiro himself.

YOSHIE: As Asata and Momota both died fairly young, the third son, Shigeharu, ended up being the sole family heir.

However, since no child lacking a left hand was born after Momota, there was no need to continue the ritual. For almost eighty years, that was the case, until

163

2006. Another was born. To my sister-in-law, Misaki.

YUZUKI: Aunt Misaki? Wait. Are you telling me that the baby she was carrying back then . . . ?

YOSHIE: That's right. The child had no left hand. They found out during her fourth-month prenatal check-up.

AUTHOR: Did the family know before it was born?

YOSHIE: Yes. Misaki actually asked me about that. She rang me one evening, and I could hear the anguish in her voice even over the telephone. 'What am I going to do, Yoshie? My baby doesn't have a left hand!' she exclaimed.

I knew what she was thinking, of course. But I never dreamt that anyone would actually go through with the Offering of the Left Hand. So, I told her not to worry and that our grandparents would never follow those old precepts.

But Misaki only grew angry. She said, 'You don't understand anything, Yoshie. You don't know what they're like!' Now, of course, I know better.

From what I heard later, it seems that the day after that telephone call, my grandparents confined Misaki to their house.

AUTHOR: Confined?!

YOSHIE: They only let her free a month later, after she had passed the twenty-second week of pregnancy. Which is the legal limit for an abortion.

AUTHOR: They wanted to keep her from seeking an abortion to avoid the ritual.

YOSHIE: Apparently so. When I heard that, it literally gave me a chill. They were serious about the Offering of the Left

164

Hand. Since he learnt it directly from Soichiro, I think Shigeharu in particular was a true believer. He feared Ushio's curse, in truth.

AUTHOR: I know they say that the child is the father of the man, but it's hard to believe that he could have gone on believing something so delusional for decades like that.

YOSHIE: I think there's a reason for it. The Katabuchi family still owned quite a bit of land apart from the manor, and with land prices skyrocketing after the war and during Japan's economic bubble, they ended up earning back quite a sizeable fortune. That meant that Shigeharu never had to find a job. He spent most of his life in that house, surrounded by the same people, with almost no contact with the outside world. And with relatives and acquaintances all benefiting from the renewed Katabuchi family fortune, no one dared oppose him or argue with him. He never had a chance to learn other ways of thinking.

AUTHOR: I see.

YOSHIE: So, Misaki was basically forced to have her baby. She had an older son, Yoichi, who normally would have been the child's warden. But, in August of that year, he died in an accident.

YUZUKI: Mother, what do you think about that accident?

Her voice was hesitant. Yoshie sat and thought for a while before answering.

YOSHIE: A month before Yoichi died, your father said something to me.

165

'Yoshie, your grandmother on your mother's side . . . Her maiden name was Katabuchi, wasn't it?' We'd only mentioned it once, when we got engaged, but I suppose he must have remembered. Then he said we should check the family tree. 'Just to be sure.' I didn't see what he meant initially, but then we traced my family tree back, and I realized.

My grandmother, who was born Yayoi Katabuchi, was Seikichi's seventh child.

YUZUKI: What?!

YOSHIE: It was hard to believe at first. But we checked it every way we could, and it's true. I carry the blood of the branch family, which makes me a potential target for the Offering of the Left Hand. And so do my children, you and your sister. Your father was worried that someday we might be chosen as victims for the Offering.

YUZUKI: He thought that Yoichi and his brother would be forced to kill us?

YOSHIE: The possibility was small, but not zero, he said. Then, he assured me that he would take care of it. He never explained what he meant, but . . .

Yoichi's death was so suspicious. I immediately thought of your father.

I asked him about it a few days later, and he broke down crying. He admitted everything. He said, 'I did it all to protect my family.'

YUZUKI: That's crazy! He killed Yoichi and turned Ayano into a criminal, and he called it 'protecting the family'?!

YOSHIE: I think he realized that. Every day, he would sit around muttering things like, 'I could have figured something out. Why did I do it?'

As much as he regretted it, though, I could never forgive him for what he had done. There were so many other choices he could have made. But, now that I think about it, your father himself was also driven half-mad by the Katabuchi family.

When he was a child, your father was also taught the Offering. He was fed those same twisted values, so when he was desperately trying to think of a way to protect his family, he fell back on those teachings. I never told you, but the accident in which he died . . . your father hadn't been drinking. At the very end, I think the guilt finally became too much to bear, and he chose to die. I suppose I pity him now, in a way.

Yoshie sighed heavily. Then, Yuzuki spoke up in a small voice.

YUZUKI: Why did you give her up?
YOSHIE: I . . .
YUZUKI: How could you give Ayano to those people? You should have refused!
YOSHIE: He threatened us. Your grandfather . . . I don't think his threats were empty, either. I mean, he locked Misaki in her house when she was pregnant to protect that damned tradition. Rather than endangering both you and Ayano, the two of us decided that giving her to him was the only way to guarantee your survival. That's what we thought, anyway.

167

YUZUKI:     But . . . couldn't you have run away or gone to the police or something?

YOSHIE:     Of course, I wanted to do that. But, that kind of thing takes preparation. I thought if we sent your sister, it might buy us some time to work out a plan to get her back safely. But I was naive. We were being watched.

You remember that man who came to live with us after your father died? Kiyotsugu, his name was. I told you I had remarried, but that was a lie. That man was your grandmother's nephew. He said he had come to help take care of us, since your father was no longer around, but his real purpose was to keep an eye on me, to make sure I didn't get in the way. That's the kind of family the Katabuchis are.

YUZUKI:     That's—

YOSHIE:     But I'm not going to make any excuses. The fact is, we as good as abandoned Ayano.

YUZUKI:     Why didn't you send me?

YOSHIE:     What?

YUZUKI:     The precepts state only that 'a relative of similar age' must serve as the child prisoner's warden. So, it could have been me, couldn't it? Why did you choose Ayano?

Yoshie paused before answering.

YOSHIE:     That was our last little bit of resistance. You were only ten at the time. Once they started brainwashing you, their twisted worldview might take you over

168

permanently. But Ayano was twelve. Her personality was more developed, and she was able to make her own judgements at that age.

I can't really know whether it was the right decision, but your sister was able to remain herself. The truth is, she sent us a letter every month.

YUZUKI: She did?

YOSHIE: I'm sure that your grandparents read over everything she wrote, so her letters only touched on safe topics. But she always expressed her worry about us. Especially you, Yuzuki. And she told us not to tell you what had happened. She didn't want to upset you. She wrote, 'I don't want her to know anything, just to forget me somehow. I want her to be free.' She included things like that in every single letter.

YUZUKI: I had no idea.

YOSHIE: Your father wanted the same thing. He said it over and over. 'Never tell Yuzuki a word.' Your sister, your father and I . . . all the three of us ever wanted was for you to find some kind of happiness away from all of this madness.

YUZUKI: Is that why you kept it so quiet all this time?

YOSHIE: Of course. But I never really believed we could keep it up. Even if we didn't talk about it, you would surely sense something, being in that house. And that's why I acted the way I did, keeping you at distance. Making you hate me. I'm so sorry. . . .

## THE PLAN

YUZUKI:   And so . . . right now, Ayano is looking after Aunt
          Misaki's child. . . . And is she having it kill people?
          Still?
YOSHIE:   That's what I thought. Until yesterday, at least.
YUZUKI:   What?
YOSHIE:   You should read the rest of the letter.

Yuzuki's hands trembled as she held the letter up to read again.

. . . Ayano told me about the Offering of the Left Hand.
I think you must know about it, Yoshie. It's so bizarre, so
far outside normal experience that it's hard to believe it's
real. But I never once doubted Ayano as she told me about
it, tears running down her face.

She said, 'In a few years, I'm going to become a criminal.
If you have anything to do with me, the guilt could fall on
you, too. So, we should just break up now.'

Over and over, I told her we could break with tradition.
She could just run away. But she always replied, 'It's impossible.' She told me that she was always being watched and
threatened, and they would never give her a chance to
escape.

I racked my brain trying to invent a way to save her.
Eventually, I came up with a plan. It was rough and not at
all a sure thing, but I could think of no other way to keep
Ayano safe.

A few days later, I bought a ring that cost all my savings,
cheap as I now know it was, and asked Ayano to marry me.

She was confused, of course. I myself admit it was far too rushed a proposal. But our marriage was necessary for my plan to work.

I told her about the plan and over the next few weeks set about persuading her to agree to it. Finally, she did.

We got married as soon as we graduated. I ignored my parents' objections and took her name, officially becoming part of the Katabuchi family. Which, in other words, meant that I would become a warden in the Offering of the Left Hand, alongside Ayano.

When I first went to the Katabuchi house to make my greetings, I was shown to the hidden room.

There, just like Ayano had told me, I found a young boy. They called him Momoya. He had been born without a left hand and, because of that, had been consigned to a terrible fate. As soon as Misaki had given birth to Momoya, she had fled the family, so now he was essentially an orphan.

His build was not much different from other children his age, but he had an unhealthy pallor, and his expression was as blank as if it had never known emotion. You could read on his body traces of the abnormal environment in which he had grown up.

Momoya was a clever boy and responded so confidently to questions, you'd have thought him much older than his six years. But he never took any action of his own volition and never expressed any of his own feelings or desires. I once saw a programme on TV about children brought up in cults, and Momoya reminded me of them. The Katabuchi family had taken away his personality.

That evening, they threw a celebration for our marriage. The people present were Ayano's grandparents Shigeharu and Fumino, Ayano and I, and one more person: a man named Kiyotsugu.

Kiyotsugu was Fumino's nephew and the person Shigeharu trusted more than anyone in the world. In the whole family, he was also the one who did more for me than any of the others. At the time, he was around forty years old, quick to laugh but still with a strangely intimidating air about him.

I remember how, after the dinner, he came and whispered in my ear, saying, 'I know things are going to be tough for you, but do your best to make sure nothing goes wrong, for the boy's sake. That Momoya is a poor little blighter. Be good to him.'

For the next few years, until Momoya turned ten, I lived in that house and learnt the role of warden. I did as I was told, as best I could, to earn the family's trust, and I tried hard to follow their instructions.

And then, a year before the ritual was set to start, I put my plan into motion.

The first thing I did was ask Shigeharu to build us a house. The five precepts of the Offering of the Left Hand do not specify exactly where the killing must happen. My proposal was that the ritual would still be satisfied if Ayano and I lived on our own with Momoya, as long as we still had him do the killing and gave the corpse's left hand to the Katabuchi family for the offering.

In the beginning Shigeharu was reluctant, but with Kiyotsugu's help, I was able to convince him. He agreed, under two conditions: that the Katabuchi family would lead the design of the layout of the new house, and that Kiyotsugu would keep watch over us.

Once we accepted those conditions, Ayano and I were allowed to live on our own. The new house was built in Saitama Prefecture, near where Kiyotsugu lived.

Before we left, Shigeharu handed me a list.

It contained over a hundred names and addresses: all the living descendants of the Katabuchi branch family. We were to choose one of those names as our victim.

I couldn't imagine how he had managed to compile such a list. The scope of it gave me a new appreciation, and fear, of the Katabuchi family's power and influence.

We moved to our new home in Saitama in June 2016. Momoya had been born in September, ten years previously, so the Offering of the Left Hand was due to begin in around 3 months. That is, if we obeyed the Katabuchi family's orders. But I had no intention of obeying. My goal was to deceive the Katabuchis and make it through the ritual without harming a soul.

I started by looking into the situation of everyone on the list, then focused on one person: A certain T——, living in Gunma Prefecture, next to Saitama. T—— was in his twenties, getting by on part-time work and, according to his neighbours, deeply in debt.

I dropped into a bar he frequented and casually made his acquaintance. After that, I made sure to keep bumping into him at the bar, and over drinks I gradually won his confidence.

Eventually, he revealed that he owed nearly two million

yen to the bank and his temp jobs barely covered the interest. This was the opportunity I'd been waiting for.

I told him I would pay off his debt and give him five hundred thousand yen on top, if he would agree to do what I asked.

He thought I was joking at first, of course, and laughed me off. I didn't give up, though, and I finally got him to listen to me.

'It all seems shady as hell, but if there's a chance it'll change the way things are going for me, I may as well trust you,' he said.

The next thing I did was hunt down a corpse. My plan absolutely depended on me locating one.

The first place I looked was the forest at Aokigahara, the famous suicide hotspot, where I naively thought that I might just stumble across a body. But although I came across lots of items left behind by people who had ended their lives in the forest, there were no corpses to be found. I returned home, dejected.

By then, there was only one week left until we had to make the offering. If I didn't find a corpse in time, the plan would be ruined.

Just as I was getting desperate, I caught a lucky break. I heard people talking about how the head of the neighbourhood association the next block over, a single man named Kyoichi Miyae, had failed to show up for a district meeting without a word to anyone. For some reason, I couldn't stop thinking about it.

I found out Miyae's address and went to his flat. I rang the doorbell over and over, but got no answer, and so I tried the door. It was unlocked. I knew it was wrong, but I stepped inside. I saw a man on the floor.

His body was cold, and there were pills scattered on the floor around him. Clearly, he had had some condition and died trying to take his medication. It was such a perfect coincidence, as if the Devil had set it up for me.

That night, I returned to Miyae's flat with my car, collected his body and brought it to our home. The whole time, I was wondering if I could still call myself innocent. If I was caught, I knew the consequences would be serious. But I didn't see any other choice. When I got home, I cut off Miyae's hand and stored it in our freezer.

A week later, the day that the Offering of the Left Hand was supposed to happen, I went to pick up T—— in my car while Ayano made dinner. When I got back with T——, a familiar car was parked in the street in front of the house. Kiyotsugu. Luckily for me, Kiyotsugu had assured me right from the beginning he wouldn't come in the house, only watch from outside.

After that, we fed T—— dinner with plenty of drinks and soon led him out of the room to the bathroom. He hid himself there, like we'd asked.

We put Miyae's severed hand in a box and gave it to Kiyotsugu, who was waiting outside. He checked the contents, then drove off for the offering at the Katabuchi house altar.

After watching Kiyotsugu leave, I went to get T—— from his hiding place and drove him to the station. I told him to go as far away as possible and not to return to his

175

apartment for at least six months. The idea was that T——
would go 'missing' from that day on.

Afterwards, all we could think about was what would
happen if our lie were exposed. A few days later, when
Kiyotsugu came to tell us that the offering had gone
smoothly, I felt a relief unlike any I'd felt in my life. We
had pulled off the first Offering of the Left Hand without
killing anyone.

But even so, there was no pleasure in the success.

We hadn't killed anyone, but what I had done was still
a crime. Kyoichi Miyae's family had no idea he was dead
and were almost certainly still searching for him. The guilt
grew heavier day by day.

And I would have to do it three more times. Searching
for a body while worrying about the police and the
Katabuchi family had been a more terrible mental stress
than I ever imagined. And I'm sure Ayano felt the same.

But even then, there was some joy in our lives. That was
watching Momoya grow.

Ayano and I would go to his room to help him study,
play games with him and just communicate. When the
final ritual was complete, the plan was that he would be
freed from his prison room and return to the Katabuchi
house. We wanted to help him regain a bit of natural
human feeling so that, when the time came, he could live
like a normal child.

And six months after he came to live with us, we started
to see a change.

At first, he just did what he was told, like some kind
of machine, but gradually he started to express emotions

176

and desires, such as 'I want to do this some more'. Or 'I don't like that'. It took time, but he began to act like other kids his age, blushing and smiling when we praised him, or getting frustrated when he lost a game.

And then, in the second year of our new life, Ayano had a baby. We named him Hiroto.

Initially, we weren't sure about bringing a baby into this situation, but living with Momoya had kindled a wish to have our own child.

We told Momoya about Hiroto, but we kept them apart. Their environments were so different that we didn't want Momoya to be hurt seeing how Hiroto was being raised. We also made sure to keep visiting Momoya in his room just as much as before, even after Hiroto was born.

When Hiroto was around one year old, Kiyotsugu had to move from Saitama to Tokyo for work. And so, the Katabuchi family paid for us to move to a new house near his in Tokyo.

I can't say that our lives in the new Tokyo house were happy, exactly, but we were more hopeful than before. If we could just make it through the remaining offerings, we would be able to live like a normal family. Hiroto was growing by the day, and Momoya was more expressive than ever.

A brighter future was just around the corner. I believed that, truly.

Looking back, I can see how silly I was.

Disaster struck out of the blue.

One evening in July of this year, Kiyotsugu rang us at around one in the morning. 'Get over here right away.

Come in your car. And bring Ayano,' he said. His voice sounded dead. I wondered what could have made him call so late. I had a terrible foreboding.

We had never left Hiroto and Momoya alone before, but they were both fast asleep, and we thought it would be all right to go out for a little while.

Kiyotsugu didn't live so far away. It only took about ten minutes by car. When we arrived, Kiyotsugu opened the door with a blank expression. 'You got caught,' he said.

I had no idea what he meant. Kiyotsugu glared at us for a moment, then went on.

'I don't place much stock in this whole Offering of the Left Hand business. Curses, hauntings, they're all just tricks people play on themselves. But Uncle Shigeharu is different. Even old as he is, he's as scared of ghosts as a little kid. So, when it comes to the Offering, he'll pay anything, even bankrupt the whole family, to make it happen.

'And I've benefited from that. The old man has paid me good money to keep an eye on you. For me, it's just a job.

'I didn't care if you cheated, as long as you didn't get caught.

'I know all about you hunting for corpses. I told myself, what did it matter, as long as the old man got his hand. So, I played along. You needed one or two million yen, I handed it over. I was going to carry on like that to the very end. But damn it. You got caught. He found out. Look at this!'

He handed me a local Saitama newspaper. The headline read, 'Corpse with Missing Left Hand Found'. Someone had discovered Kyoichi Miyae's body.

'The old man just happened to see this. It seems the "missing left hand" part bothered him, so he started checking the list of branch family descendants and found that they were all alive and well. Uncle Shigeharu called me in and gave me the third degree. Of course, I insisted I had no idea what had happened. Now, to earn the old man's forgiveness, I have to bring Momoya to his house within the day. I suppose he's going to take charge of the rest of the Offerings himself.

'I don't know what's going to happen to you two. All I know is, if you don't take Momoya to him today, my neck's on the line. So, you're going to give me the boy. Now. Let's go.'

He took us out to his car. He got in, and we sat in the back seats.

'Right, this is what's going to happen. We're going over to your place. When we get there, you go inside and bring Momoya out to me. If you do as you're told, there's nothing to worry about. But if you give me any trouble, well . . . I think you can imagine I won't be too pleased.'

I understood then why Kiyotsugu had told us to come in our own car. It was to keep us from taking Momoya and making a run for it when we got back.

If we let Momoya go to the Katabuchi house, he would be forced to murder someone.

We sat in silence while Kiyotsugu drove, all the while talking on in a disturbingly casual tone.

'I feel sorry for poor little Momoya, I do. But this is the fate he was born to. It's a pity, but it is what it is. Right, here we are. You have ten minutes. Got that? Back here in ten.'

We got out of the car. Neither of us knew what to do. I looked up at the house and saw that the lights were on in our bedroom. We had turned all the lights off when we left. Thinking that Hiroto must have woken up, we rushed to the second-floor bedroom.

When we got there, we were shocked at what we saw. Momoya was sitting on Hiroto's bed, and I was suddenly overcome with fear.

Momoya's bedroom door was always locked from the outside. But there was another way out, which the Katabuchi family had included in the house plans. A hidden passage between his room and the bathroom. He could also get into the rest of the house that way.

The door was hidden by a set of shelves, but Momoya might still have discovered it. When he realized we had gone out, had he taken his chance to escape and attack Hiroto?

Chills ran through my whole body.

But when I rushed over to the bed to stop Momoya, I realized I had been totally wrong.

A damp cloth had been folded up and placed neatly on Hiroto's forehead. I saw it was a towel from Momoya's room.

And finally, finally, I understood.

Occasionally, Hiroto would wake up in the middle of the night with a fever. It must have happened after we had gone out. Momoya had heard him crying and, realizing something was wrong, got out of his room to see what was the matter. Then, he had carefully dampened and folded that towel, despite his missing hand, and tended to Hiroto.

When we asked him, Momoya admitted that he'd known about the passage for a while. He sometimes used it to get out late at night and watch Hiroto sleeping.

I was filled with regret for doubting Momoya, even for a moment. And for letting my fear of the Katabuchis drive me to locking him up in that room and forcing him to live such a dark little life.

He had done nothing to deserve being treated like that. I begged Momoya's forgiveness, over and over again. Ayano was crying, as well.

We heard footsteps in the corridor, then Kiyotsugu came in.

'I've been waiting long enough!' he growled. He grabbed Momoya and dragged him out of the room. I had the feeling that if I let them get away, we would never see Momoya again. He would live the rest of his life with the guilt of having killed someone. If indeed the Katabuchis let him live after the offerings were finished, of which there was no guarantee.

I had no time to think. I have chosen the only way to make sure this all ends.

I'm sorry for rambling on and making you read all this. Right now, Ayano is living with Hiroto and Momoya in flat number X at ——.

There doesn't seem to be anything else I can do to protect my family now. Ayano is working part-time at a supermarket near their flat but makes barely enough to get by on.

I know that this is far too much to ask, but if there is any way you could help to support the three of them, I would be more grateful than I could say. Please.

With deepest respect,

Keita Katabuchi

Yoshie picked up a newspaper that had been sitting on the sofa next to her and spread it out on the table. 'I suppose you haven't read this yet?'

It was the evening edition from the 25th of October. It must have just been delivered.

'MAN WANTED FOR MURDER OF IN-LAWS'

On 25th October, the Metropolitan Police announced that Keita Katabuchi of ——, Tokyo, is wanted on suspicion of murder. An arrest warrant was issued for Katabuchi regarding the July murder of his father-in-law, Shigeharu Katabuchi, and Shigeharu's nephew, Kiyotsugu Morigaki. The suspect's whereabouts are currently unknown. . . .

YUZUKI: So, right now, Keita is . . . ?

YOSHIE: It seems he's gone on the run. I think he's trying to take all the blame himself.

YUZUKI: I can't . . . but . . . why did he go so far as all this?

YOSHIE: I know. It's hard for me to believe, too. But I think I understand now what he meant when he wrote about choosing the only way to make sure this all ends. He is trying to protect Ayano and the children.

YUZUKI: That may be so, but . . . I don't think he can go on running forever, and when they catch him, it's only going
to make things worse.

YOSHIE: You're right. For now, I'm doing everything I can to be
ready to make things easier if that happens. But there's
something I'd like to ask of you, Yuzuki. It's to do with
your sister.

YUZUKI: Is she all right?

YOSHIE: She's fine. We just talked on the phone, actually.
She's in low spirits, as you'd imagine, but for now
all three of them are healthy. They're still living in
the flat Keita mentioned in his letter. So, what I'd
like to ask, Yuzuki, is that you find some way to help
your sister. I'll take care of the money side, but I
need you to be their emotional support. All three of
them. You're the one that Ayano most wants to see
right now.

After that, Yuzuki and her mother left for the flat where Ayano
and her family were staying.

They invited me along, but of course it would be no place for
outsiders. I politely declined.

When we said goodbye, Yuzuki bowed and thanked me repeat-
edly, much to my embarrassment.

.     .     .

After a police investigation and statements from multiple witnesses, the following has become clear:

183

- The bodies of Shigeharu Katabuchi and Kiyotsugu Morigaki were found deep in the mountains of —— Prefecture. The two had been dead approximately three months.
- Shigeharu's wife, Fumino, was found to be suffering from profound dementia and was placed in a home for the elderly in —— Prefecture.
- Misaki Katabuchi remains missing. One reported sighting of someone resembling her in an —— Prefecture convenience store is yet to be confirmed. The police investigation is ongoing.

·    ·    ·

I hope this finds you well. This is Yuzuki Katabuchi.

Once more, please let me tell you how much I appreciate all your help.

I'm writing because I wanted to let you know how things have been going since that day.

At the moment, Ayano, Hiroto and Momoya are staying with my mother.

Mother seems to be enjoying life with her two new grandchildren and is much more cheerful than ever before.

Ayano is working part-time and studying for her child caregiver certification.

None of us knows what the future holds.

Keita is still missing, and the worry of it is terrible, but we are all doing our best to remain cheerful and have fun for the children's sake.

When things finally settle down, I would like to meet up and thank you properly.

Please also convey my regards to Mr Kurihara.

Yuzuki Katabuchi

.　.　.

A few days later, I visited Kurihara at his Umegaoka flat and related all that had happened.

KURIHARA: Aha. So, that's what was going on. There was a lot more to it than I'd imagined. I suppose I wasn't much help, after all.

AUTHOR: That's not true! Ms Katabuchi is grateful, too. You helped us understand so much.

KURIHARA: You think so? Well, I suppose now we can just sit back and watch what unfolds from the outside.

Kurihara took a sip of coffee.

KURIHARA: But I wonder who the other one was?

AUTHOR: Other one . . . what?

KURIHARA: The other murdered child of the Katabuchi branch family. Yoshie said Rankyo had Momota kill three children, right? His firstborn from his first wife, and the third and fourth sons, born of his third wife.

But, if they were strictly following the rules of the Offering of the Left Hand, the boy was supposed to kill a child every year from his tenth to his thirteenth birthday. Ten, eleven, twelve, thirteen. One child a year makes four children. So, who's the final victim?

AUTHOR:    Hmm . . . maybe they gave up partway? Yoshie said that it's possible Seikichi's family noticed and cut off all ties.

KURIHARA:    If they'd noticed, do you really think they'd stop at 'cutting off all ties'?

Besides. Soichiro drummed the Offering of the Left Hand into his children for the future, even after Momota's was over. Someone so fixated on the ritual wouldn't have abandoned it before completion.

AUTHOR:    I see. . . .

KURIHARA:    Yeah, I'm sure there must have been a fourth victim.

AUTHOR:    But surely Seikichi would have noticed four of his children being murdered?

KURIHARA:    Don't be so sure he didn't.

AUTHOR:    What do you mean?

KURIHARA:    It's possible he noticed but let it happen. You've heard of *mabiki*?

*Mabiki*. 'Thinning the garden'. In Japan, there was once a tradition of aborting babies or even killing children to keep down the number of mouths to feed. The practice lasted into the late nineteenth or even early twentieth century in some communities.

AUTHOR:    But that was something poor families did when they couldn't afford to feed all their children, right? What reason could Seikichi have had for it, with all his wealth?

KURIHARA:    *Mabiki* wasn't limited to the poor. Seikichi had several wives, and they were always competing with each other. Their animosity must have grown so great that Seikichi himself couldn't control it. So, he might have thought the cost of a few children was worth it to keep his wives from turning on him, as well. . . . Anyway, this is all just speculation.

AUTHOR: Let's put that to rest. It's all ancient history. Seikichi is dead, so there's no use in thinking about it anyway.

KURIHARA: I suppose you're right. So, let's talk about today. There's actually one more thing that's bothering me.

It's that list Shigeharu gave to Keita. The one with over a hundred names of branch family descendants. How on earth did he get that information?

AUTHOR: Well, I mean . . . the two branches of the family were connected, after all. There must have been some records. . . .

KURIHARA: But they officially fractured into two families decades ago. And after the war, Seikichi's descendants were scattered all over Japan. As a member of the head family, Shigeharu wouldn't have access to the branch family records, so tracking down all their names and addresses would be nearly impossible.

AUTHOR: Then, how did he do it?

KURIHARA: There must have been someone feeding information to the main family.

AUTHOR: Like a mole, you mean?

KURIHARA: That's right. I think the only person who could manage to track down all of the descendants would be a member of the Seikichi branch. In other words, a descendant of Seikichi Katabuchi was giving information to the main family, despite the apparent enmity.

AUTHOR:    Who on earth would do that?

KURIHARA:  There's one person who springs to mind. Someone who is both descended from Seikichi and connected to the main family. Yoshie.

AUTHOR:    What?!

KURIHARA:  Yoshie said her grandmother was Seikichi's seventh child, Yayoi, didn't she?

AUTHOR:    Yes, she did. . . .

KURIHARA:  How's this for a theory? The fourth victim of the Offering of the Left Hand was Yayoi's brother. Yayoi swore revenge on the Katabuchi house for her brother's murder. Just like Soichiro, Yayoi put a kind of curse on her own children. 'You must kill members of the Katabuchi head family.'

It was passed down through the generations, all the way to Yoshie. Then, she married into the head family. I wonder if that was just a coincidence. Perhaps Yoichi's death, her husband's accident and Keita's rebellion were all part of her plan.

I was about to say, 'That's impossible!' but then I stopped to think. Kurihara's reasoning was ridiculous. It was out of the question. But the fact remained that there were a few things about Yoshie that bothered me, too.

When talking about Rankyo, she'd said, 'I used my own ways to look into this Rankyo's story.' What did she mean, 'my own ways'?

And that old bundle of paper with the five precepts of the Offering of the Left Hand. That was surely one of the head family's most prized possessions. How had Yoshie got hold of it?

188

Also, now that I think of it . . . Misaki was locked up the morning after she called Yoshie. The next morning! Was that a coincidence, too?

Here's another thing: Shigeharu apparently read about the discovery of Kyoichi Miyae's body in a local Saitama newspaper, but Shigeharu didn't live anywhere near Saitama. How did he get hold of it?

As the questions mounted up, my head started to spin.

At the same time, I remembered the sight of Yoshie weeping as she confessed all her regrets to her daughter . . . that couldn't have been a performance, could it? But then . . .

AUTHOR: No . . . there's no way.

KURIHARA: Anyway, it's all just pure speculation. Don't pay me any mind.

Kurihara flashed a broad grin and drained his coffee cup. I felt a twinge of irritation at his total lack of concern.

# AFTERWORD

## Kurihara

I first met Uketsu in 2018. He sought me out as a consultant for a story involving architecture. In the end, that particular story never came out, but from that first meeting we've worked together on several other projects of his. Keeping in mind that I use the term 'worked' very loosely here.

I had the opportunity to review those stories and books at the manuscript stage, and one thing I can say about all of them is, each one contains a lie. Well, that might be an exaggeration.

Out of respect for Uketsu's good name, I'll clarify that none of the stories include anything that is not based entirely on fact.

However, there are points where the truth is left out. In other words, Uketsu's work omits things that actually happened.

However, I am not trying to accuse Uketsu of dishonesty or deception. When writing articles for a mass audience, you have to leave out a certain amount of information.

Let me give you an example.

Today is Taro's mother's birthday. Taro went to buy her a piece of cake. On the way, he noticed a glove left on the pavement. When he got to the shop, he saw they had some delicious-looking cake, but he didn't have enough money to buy it. So, he had to buy a cheaper cake that didn't look as good. On the way home, Taro was sad that he hadn't been able to buy something better, but his mother smiled as she ate the cake and told him it how much she enjoyed it. That cheered him up.

The mention of the glove is clearly immaterial to the story. In fact, it's a bit of a tease that could get readers confused trying to figure out what a glove dropped in the street has to do with cake. And so, if you were going to tell someone this story, you'd omit the glove part, making it a very pleasant little story about the love between Taro and his mother. And yet, if there is even the tiniest chance that the glove does, in fact, have something to do with the true import of what happened that day, then the reader will be robbed of the chance to know that from the start.

If I am totally honest, Uketsu has omitted a 'glove' from *Strange Houses*. At the end of the story, there is a scene where I speculate about Yoshie (and to tell the truth, I was a little bit hurt when I later read about Uketsu's irritation). At the time, I actually went a bit further in my speculation, but Uketsu chose not to include that part. I can only assume that was out of concern for the people involved.

I can understand that concern, but at this point, I think enough time has passed to ease the worry. So, I will tack on my speculation here.

.   .   .

Looking at the Tokyo house floor plan, you can see a small window in the wall between the first-floor bedroom and the living room. It is very rare to see such windows in bedrooms, because they destroy privacy. So, why include one?

In light of the condition that 'the Katabuchi family would lead the design of the layout', it's natural to assume that window was the family's idea.

The base assumption when designing the layout was that the house would be used for murder. This bedroom would have been for the poor victim. In which case, the (simple) logical explanation would be that the window was a way for the murderers—Keita and Ayano—to observe their target from the living room. However, as anyone who has now read the whole story should understand, there was no need to observe this room, because the victim would have been murdered in the bathroom, before they ever entered the bedroom.

So, what if we change our thinking? In the condition 'the Katabuchi family would lead the design of the layout', the word 'family' should be paid particular attention. It's the family, not just one person. As family members, Keita and Ayano could have had some input. If we allow for that possibility, then why might the couple want this small window added? Let's look at a quote from me in this very book:

KURIHARA: Remember the bedroom on the first floor? I do still think it was used for guests, but I imagine that, most of the time, the father slept there. The family regularly killed people. That could also mean their own lives were sometimes in danger. I'm thinking that the father must have seen his role as defender of the castle, to keep his wife and son from harm, so he slept down on the first floor to be close to the entrance.

If we follow my past thinking, then perhaps that window would have allowed Keita to keep an eye on the living room from his bedroom. I can't say for sure if that's correct or not. Keita and Ayano didn't actually kill anyone—or, rather, strictly speaking, they resisted to the very end carrying out the murders that the Katabuchi family ordered—and they never wanted to. Which would mean they didn't need to be on the lookout for anyone sneaking in to take revenge.

So, what was the window for? From here, I'd like to speculate a little more freely.

What if we combine elements of those two different theories: the small window was there to allow observation of the bedroom. The bedroom was there for Keita.

So, the window was there so Ayano could watch Keita from outside. You might think that sounds absurd, and that would be entirely natural. Keita and Ayano were a happy couple and working together to oppose the Katabuchi family. Why would such a couple take on roles like observer/observed? It's unthinkable.

But that's only if we believe everything that Keita wrote in his letter.

From the beginning, though, there was never any reason for Keita to get involved in this horrific Katabuchi family story. Even so, Keita seems to have freely thrown himself into it for one reason: he loved Ayano.

Now, there certainly are those who swear by the 'power of love', but I have my doubts. I wonder, would anyone really

196

sacrifice their whole future for a school sweetheart? I think, instead, that Keita was also a prisoner, unable to escape.

Lastly, this might be entirely uncalled for, but with the final events of the case now two months behind us, we still don't know where Keita is. We also, coincidentally, still don't know the identity of that dismembered body found in the brush in Tokyo that showed up in chapter one.

Of course, like I said, this is pure speculation, and I have no proof. But, in much the same way, there is no proof that it was Keita who actually wrote that letter.

# ABOUT THE AUTHOR

Uketsu only ever appears online, wearing a mask and speaking through a voice changer.

He has more than 1.5 million followers.

His innovative 'sketch mysteries' challenge readers to discover the hidden clues in a series of sinister drawings.

They have sold nearly 3 million copies in Japan since 2021.

Translation rights have been sold in twenty-seven languages and counting.

Uketsu's true name and identity remain unknown.

# A NOTE FROM THE TRANSLATOR

I first read *Strange Houses* in 2022, not long after finishing my translation of *The Devil's Flute Murders* by Seishi Yokomizo. Anyone who has read both might well recognize certain connections between the two—both in atmosphere and distinct plot points—and I immediately sensed that this rapidly rising star, Uketsu, was worth watching. I could see both that his writing was obviously and intentionally open to readers of all stripes, with a priority on accessibility and clarity, while still respecting the tropes and traditions of mystery and horror fiction in Japan. That is what attracted my initial attention, but it was not until I read *Strange Pictures* that I was convinced that these books would be perfect for English translation. And, well, here we are.

The stated intent behind all the pictures and diagrams in Uketsu's books is to lower the barrier to entry, so that his often quite intricate explanations and tricks remain understandable even to younger readers. His language is clear, precise, and unembellished, without particularly difficult sentence structure or wording. Which is not to say that there is no depth to the story, because there is. Surprising depth, given the emphasis on accessible reading experiences. In Uketsu's work, I think, much of it is found in what is left unsaid and unexplained, those liminal spaces where the imagination is encouraged to wander. For, while there is a lot of explanation in these books, there is always room left to ask, "Is that all?" Because it almost certainly isn't. I mean, who actually was that dead body in the first chapter?

Still, all told, I could not ask for a friendlier text as a translator. There were points where I struggled to find the proper English for a given term or concept, but never any where I struggled to understand what Uketsu was trying to say or what kind of experience he was trying to offer to his readers, because it was all served up so kindly. It is that experience of *Strange Houses* I most wanted to bring out in my translation, rather than sticking too tightly to the wording or sentence level, and all my translation decisions went to serve it. And what an experience it is!

It starts out with something utterly confounding—a dismembered body in the bushes. It grows more outlandish, with speculation on murder houses and children forced to dismember strangers, only for the denouement to wrap it all up in a nice, if utterly bizarre, package—which then gets unraveled by a few offhand comments from Kurihara.

In prioritizing that experience, though, I had to be careful not to spoil surprises. I had to remember, as someone who had read the book time after time in the process of translation, that new readers should remain in the dark about nearly everything. Take, for example, the identity of Yuzuki Miyae/Katabuchi. Early on, he makes a comment that, if examined too deeply, would be odd for someone hoping to find her husband's murderer but totally understandable for someone worried that her sister was living in a murder house. Making that comment too natural would erode any incongruity but making it too obvious might clue people in to things too early. Each new twist of the story, each loose end tied up just before each new outlandish development, adds fresh